DEFENDING CHAMP

DEFENDING CHAMP

CHAMP

MIKE LUPICA

Philomel Books

PHILOMEL BOOKS
An imprint of Penguin Random House LLC, New York

First published in the United States of America by Philomel Books,
an imprint of Penguin Random House LLC, 2021

Visit us online at penguinrandomhouse.com.

Library of Congress Cataloging-in-Publication Data is available.

Printed in the USA

ISBN 9781984836922

LSCH

1 3 5 7 9 10 8 6 4 2

Edited by Dana Leydig
Text set in Life BT

This book is for two amazing women who understand
Alex Carlisle completely, and have informed her strength
and spirit and humor and intelligence:

My wife, Taylor.
And my daughter, Hannah Grace.

PROLOGUE

IT'S ME AGAIN.

Seventh grader Alex Carlisle.

The girl who got to play quarterback last year on the Orville Middle School boys' football team.

Except I never thought of it that way. As *their* team.

Just ours.

Bottom line? I learned so much last season. Not just about friendship or what it takes to be a good teammate. But about overcoming fears and chasing dreams. I'd started out thinking I wanted to prove a point to all the people who doubted me. Who doubted that a girl could play what had always been a "boys-only" sport.

It was way bigger than that, though. I proved a point to *myself* and learned a lesson I'll never forget. That if you've got the talent and the belief in yourself, all you need to achieve great things—in sports or anything else—is this:

A chance.

But it turns out my story didn't end with the football season.

No. In fact, that was only the beginning . . .

1

IT WAS CHRISTMAS EVE, AND ALEX AND HER DAD WERE SPRAWLED out on the couch, watching the Steelers play their last game of the regular season.

They had to start their backup quarterback today, but if they won, they were back in the playoffs.

"I started out as a backup to Jeff Stiles," Alex said to Jack Carlisle, "and look how well things worked out for me."

Her dad smiled at her. That smile had always made her feel like being wrapped in a soft blanket.

"I never thought of you as second-string," he said, "not from the moment you made that team."

Alex rolled her eyes playfully. "You're my dad," she said. "It's not like you were impartial or anything."

"But you know better than anyone that *I* know my football," he said. "And once I saw you on that field, throwing the ball the way you'd done in our backyard, I knew I was looking at the best QB your age in Orville."

Alex smiled back at him. The day before Christmas was always a special day in the Carlisle household. And watching football with her dad was like an early holiday present. She just wished the Steelers were playing at home this week, so that instead of the couch, they could sit in their reserved seats at Heinz Field.

Jack had bought season tickets the year Alex was born. It was like he predicted his daughter would one day grow up to be as big a Steelers fan as he was.

"You honestly thought that?" Alex asked. "Even though there'd never been a girl on the team before?"

"Of course," he said, without a hint of hesitation. "I knew I was looking at a quarterback. And somebody who had a passion for football since you were old enough to attend your first game."

"Like I had a choice," she said.

"And what *would* you have chosen if I hadn't given you a little nudge in the direction of Heinz Field?" he said.

"Little?" Alex said with a sideways glance.

"Answer the question."

"I would have chosen Section 136, visitors' side of the stadium."

It was where their seats were located. And Alex knew that even with the snow coming down the way it was now, they would have braved the cold if in fact the Steelers *were* playing at home. But as far as Alex was concerned, the snow made today even more special. There'd be snow on the ground when she woke tomorrow morning, and Christmas would look exactly how she thought it should in their part of the world. Sometimes she couldn't believe it was only a little over a month ago that she'd achieved her dream of playing starting quarterback for the Owls, making things just about perfect in *her* world.

Not totally perfect, of course.

She always missed her mom during the holidays. Her parents had divorced a long time ago, but remained close friends, and Alex still talked to her mom regularly over the phone. But Dr. Liza Borelli now lived in San Francisco with her husband, Richard, and Alex's five-year-old half brother, Connor. Alex's mom had decided to pursue her own dream of becoming a doctor, and over time, Alex had come to understand that sacrifice. Especially during the last few months. Because now, more than ever, Alex understood how it felt to chase a dream.

In fact, Alex's football playing had only served to strengthen their relationship, which was ironic since Jack often joked that his ex-wife knew less about football than he knew about pediatric surgery. But through their shared experiences of defying the odds and overcoming unfair obstacles, Alex and her mom began to see each other a little more clearly.

Even with this newfound mother-daughter bond, Alex knew the hurt from her parents' divorce would never fully disappear. But having experienced the struggles she did just to play football, and knowing what it had cost her, she'd learned a lot about choices. Especially for women.

Around halftime, Alex and her dad headed to the kitchen to start preparing dinner. Today, her job was to chop vegetables for the pasta primavera, while her dad boiled a pot of water and started heating up the sauce. The kitchen may not have been Alex's favorite place in the world, but being close to her dad certainly was.

While he kept an eye on the pasta he'd just thrown into the pot on the stove, he started assembling the salad. Alex knew he was a bear for making salads and tossing in as much fresh produce as possible. Jack belonged to the local CSA, or community-supported agriculture, and got a weekly delivery of fresh fruits and vegetables to use in their daily meals. Alex had to hand it to him—he'd become an ace at cooking for two. No thanks to Alex, of course, but she helped where she could.

Jack liked to sum up his philosophy in the kitchen this way:

"Go big or go home."

Alex would usually respond by saying, "Dad? You *are* home."

There was still some time before halftime was over. He had collected the veggies now and began cooking them up in a frying pan.

"So," he said, "have you given any thought to what you want to do in the spring? Sports-wise, I mean."

"*Dad*," she said. "Football ended, like, yesterday." She pointed out the kitchen window, where the snow was coming down even harder now, already covering the backyard in a sheet of white. "And you may have noticed that *winter* just officially started."

"And *you*, young lady, may have noticed that *I* like to plan ahead," Jack replied.

"Huh," Alex said. "Never picked up on that."

Because she knew him as well as she did, she'd been expecting the question.

"All I know is that I'm not going to play a winter sport," Alex said. "Football was pretty intense, all the way to the last minute of the last game. Think I could use a break."

"The reason I bring it up," her dad said, "is because I was thinking of maybe hiring a coach to give you some private quarterbacking lessons. That's if you still want to play football next year."

"*Totally* going out for football next year," Alex said without missing a beat.

"So how would you feel about a private coach?"

"I don't know." Alex shrugged. "I mean, aren't *you* my private coach?"

Her dad had once been a star quarterback at Orville High.

"I'm talking about a trained professional," Jack said. "Someone who can really coach you up, work with you one on one, perfect your form."

Alex thought for a moment. It would be nice to get the help. Then she could come back next season and surprise everyone with her improvement.

But when she really considered it, she knew it wasn't what she really wanted. There was something else she craved. Something she'd been missing.

"If I am going to do something in the spring, I want to be on a team," she said. "I realized that during football. Even when most of the other players didn't want me there."

"Problem is," he said, "football is a fall sport."

Now was as good a time as any to tell him, she thought.

"Well, not *all* kinds of football," she said, a little coy.

Jack looked up from stirring the pot of pasta. "Not sure I'm following," he said. "But you know I'm a little slow out of the chutes sometimes."

"Well, you know how they call soccer 'football' pretty much everywhere else in the world," Alex said. "And the school offers spring soccer, so . . ."

From the living room they heard the announcers come on

again, signaling the beginning of the second half.

"Wait," he said, "am I hearing you right? You want to go back to your old team?"

They left the sauce to simmer and drained the pasta before making their way back to the living room, planting themselves in their usual spots on the couch.

"Umm," Alex said. "Maybe?"

"As I recall," Jack said, "you were about as popular with your former teammates as you were with the guys on the football team at the start of the season. And well *into* the season, I might add. You sure you wanna do this? I mean, I'd support you either way, but—"

"Not saying I'm going to do it for sure," she said. "Just something I've been thinking about."

The Steelers and Bengals were lining up now for the second-half kickoff.

Her dad pulled her close to him and kissed the top of her head.

"Apparently I'm not the only one who plans ahead," he said.

THEY WERE BACK IN THE KITCHEN NOW. ALEX RINSED OFF THEIR dinner plates before placing them in the dishwasher, while Jack wiped off the counter.

The Steelers won on a field goal with three seconds left in the game. It was a close finish, but any time the Steelers eked out a win, it was cause for celebration.

Dessert tonight was Alex's favorite: brownie, vanilla ice cream on top, fudge sauce on top of that, and a sprinkling of mini M&M's.

"Can we talk a little more about soccer?" Jack said as they sat down at the kitchen table. "Just in light of how mean some of those girls were to my kid?"

"Not all of them," Alex said. "Annie Burgess was pretty cool."

"Okay, so *most* of them," Jack said. "If you do decide to go back—"

"Haven't decided that," Alex reminded him.

"But if you do," he said, "how do you think they'll react?"

It was something Alex had considered. The main thing, really.

"Trust me, Dad," Alex said, "I've been asking myself the same question."

There was a brief pause while Alex took a bite of brownie. She swallowed, wiped her face, then continued. "Remember what you said about the guys coming around because I gave them a better chance to win?"

Jack only nodded, urging her to continue.

"I don't want to sound cocky . . . but I was a pretty good center middie."

"Better than pretty good," her dad said.

"On the other hand," Alex said, "the fall team did make it to the championship game without me . . ."

Alex's dad's eyes were on the TV, but he nodded pensively. "They're a strong team," he agreed. "No doubt about that. But you're a strong player. They'd be foolish not to accept you back."

"*If* I decide to go back," Alex added.

"Right," he said. "Big if."

There was plenty to consider. First, whether she'd be allowed back onto the team. And second, whether she was ready to face her peers again. Or at least one in particular.

"Yeah, I'm sure Lindsey Stiles will welcome me back with open arms," Alex said with an extremely heavy dose of sarcasm.

They both knew that Lindsey, whose cousin, Jeff, Alex had beaten out for the quarterback position, had been the one leading the charge against Alex for quitting soccer last season.

"But Annie will be there too," Alex reasoned. "She stuck up for me, big-time. And got elected captain of that team despite Lindsey practically campaigning for the job."

Her dad grinned.

"You're pretty popular with the Stiles family," he said. "We should have them over for dinner sometime."

Alex's eyes strayed from the TV over to her dad, and they

shared a good laugh at her dad's heavy dose of sarcasm.

"Listen," he said, "the good thing is that you don't have to decide any of this on Christmas Eve."

"I know," she said. "I just think it would be cool to be back running around with my old teammates when Orville finally thaws out."

"And who knows," her dad said, "by then, maybe those teammates will have thawed out too."

They cleaned the kitchen and then went back into the living room to watch the Chiefs and the Ravens play. No better quarterbacking show on Earth, as far as Alex was concerned. Patrick Mahomes against Lamar Jackson. Both of them could run up and down the field and complete crazy passes like they were making everything up on the fly. She settled in at her end of the couch, totally content to watch another game. Her football season might be over, but the NFL's sure wasn't. For this one night, soccer could wait.

At the end of the second quarter, the score was tied at 24-all, so Jack got up from his end of the couch and walked over to the Christmas tree the two of them had picked out together. Then he knelt down and shifted a few boxes around before returning with one he'd wrapped—badly, as usual—plus a plain white envelope that had *Alex* written on the outside in his messy scrawl.

"Couple of early presents," he said, handing them to Alex.

"No way!" Alex yelled, sitting up straighter in her seat. "You *always* make me wait until Christmas morning."

He shrugged. "You think you're the only one who can call an audible?"

Alex set the box on her lap and began tearing open the wrapping paper. She opened the top, and inside was a regulation NFL football, with two autographs written on it in black permanent marker.

Terry Bradshaw's was one.

Ben Roethlisberger's was the other.

Since there was no bigger Steelers fan than Alex Carlisle, she knew full well that her team had won six Super Bowls in their history. Bradshaw had been the quarterback for four of them, back in the 1970s. Ben Roethlisberger had quarterbacked the team for the other two.

Alex opened her mouth wide enough to swallow the ball whole.

"*How* . . . both of them?!"

"I know people," her dad said, "who know people."

She jumped toward her dad and hugged him so hard she nearly knocked him over the arm of the sofa.

"How many times do I have to tell you?" he said. "No tackle football in the house."

"Thank you so, so, so, *soooooo* much," Alex said.

"Autographs from our two champion quarterbacks," he said, "for *my* championship quarterback."

She sat there for a few minutes staring at the football in her hands, occasionally gripping it as if she were about to throw a tight spiral down the field. She ran a finger across the signatures, still finding it hard to believe her dad had pulled this off. Perhaps it was a Christmas miracle.

"You're not done," her dad said finally, and nodded at the envelope on the coffee table.

When Alex ripped the envelope open, there was an official-looking certificate inside.

FOR ALEX CARLISLE was printed at the top in block letters. Underneath, at the very bottom, Jack had signed his name.

But at the center of the document, big and bold, were the letters IOU.

"You owe me what?" Alex said, cutting her dad a curious glance.

"Can't tell you," he said. "At least not yet."

It wasn't like Jack to be so mysterious, and Alex was sufficiently stumped. She wondered briefly what sort of surprise he was planning but decided not to drive herself nuts trying to figure it out. If she knew her dad, it would be worth the wait.

Instead, she got up and tossed the signed football to her dad, who stood over by the tree. He caught it and tossed it back, before falling back onto the couch for the second half of the game. Then they sat together, with the TV on, and Alex was as happy as she'd ever been.

"A signed football and a surprise," she said, the football beside her. "This is already the best Christmas ever."

"And it isn't even Christmas yet," he said.

She turned away from the TV just briefly to glance out the window and watch the snowflakes drift down into their front yard.

"All of a sudden," Alex said, "I've got the feeling this year might be even more *full* of surprises than last year."

"The good kind of surprises, I hope."

"Totally."

Neither one of them had any idea.

ALEX HAD INVITED HER BEST FRIEND, SOPHIE LYONS, OVER FOR A sleepover on New Year's Eve. Gabe Hildreth and Jabril Wise, both football teammates, were her best guy friends. But Sophie was in a class of her own.

When most of the other girls in their grade had turned their backs on Alex after she'd tried out for football, Sophie was one of the only ones who hadn't. In fact, just the opposite. Sophie not only took Alex's side, but fought on her behalf and supported Alex every step of the way.

Sophie was captain of the cheerleading team at school. But during the last football season, it was as if her main job was cheering on *Alex*. Or at least that's the way it seemed from Alex's spot on the field.

Sophie had just come back from a skiing trip to Vermont with her family over Christmas and was now home until school opened again in January. So it was a party for two tonight, both of them excited to stay up until midnight and toast the New Year with sparkling cider and noisemakers.

They'd popped popcorn in the microwave and were eating it out of a big bowl between them on Alex's bed. It was still a few hours until the ball dropped, so they filled the time watching funny videos on their phones and chatting about what they planned to do during the rest of the holiday break.

"I know what I'm going to do," Sophie said. "Train."

"You already train harder than anybody," Alex said. "And you're the star of your team."

Sophie just shrugged. "You're never really done training," she said. "There's always room to improve. Plus I really want to make nationals this year."

It wasn't the first time Sophie had mentioned this particular cheerleading competition. The one that took place annually at the Walt Disney World Resort in Orlando. Sophie thought her team was strong enough to make the cut this year for their age bracket.

"People have no idea how hard we work," Sophie said. "They think all we do is cheer at football games and shake pom-poms, but it's so much more than that. We practice three hours a day, perfecting our routines, practicing stunts, tumbling across the mat. It's a lot."

"You don't have to tell me," Alex said. "I could barely manage one afternoon of your 'coaching.' "

Sophie held in a laugh, but Alex remembered the day well. Toe-touches and high Vs and heel stretches—even just keeping up with the terminology was exhausting.

They were getting low on popcorn, but that hardly mattered. There was more in the kitchen, and they both knew it wouldn't be their last bowl tonight.

"What do you mean by 'train,' exactly?" Alex asked now. "Is that different from practice?"

Sophie nodded. "I'm back with my old gym coach, Mrs.

Santos," she said. "She's been helping me incorporate more gymnastics into my cheerleading. My cheer coaches have even started letting me help choreograph some of our halftime routines."

Sophie beamed with pride. Alex wasn't entirely sure what that meant, but if Sophie's expression was anything to go on, it must have been a pretty big deal.

"That's awesome, Soph!" Alex said. "You're, like, the Simone Biles of cheerleading!"

Simone Biles, they both knew, was one of the greatest gymnasts and Olympic athletes of all time. Even though she was only four feet eight, she went on to win thirty medals, including four gold in the summer Olympic Games. Alex's dad had always told her, from the first time she started playing sports, that size absolutely mattered:

The size of your talent and the size of your heart.

Sophie had both in abundance. But the size of her dream was even bigger.

Alex had her own dream, of course. One that'd required her to leave soccer, and one that involved coming back to it. Go figure.

"If I keep getting better," Sophie said, "so will our team. The other girls want the cheerleading championship as much as I do." She smiled sheepishly. "Well, almost."

They had talked about putting on a movie while they waited for the ball to drop in Times Square, but ultimately decided against it. One thing was always true when Alex Carlisle and Sophie Lyons were together: they never ran out of things to talk about.

Sophie tossed a piece of popcorn into the air, caught it in her mouth.

"So my big New Year's resolution is about the cheerleading finals," Sophie said. "What's yours?"

"It's not a goal, exactly," Alex said, sitting up cross-legged on her bed. "More like an idea."

"I better be the first to know."

"Will you settle for the second to know?" she said. "'Cause I already told my dad."

Sophie blinked dramatically. "I *suppose* I can live with that."

Alex took a deep breath. "Okay, here goes," she said. "My resolution is to be brave and be bold."

Sophie paused and tilted her head, as if in deep thought.

"I knew it," Alex said. "You think it's weird."

"Then you obviously don't know me at all," Sophie said. "Because I think it's awesome. In fact, I might borrow it and make it one of my own resolutions."

"Why not?" Alex said. "You're always borrowing my clothes."

"Which reminds me," Sophie said, "got anything new for me to try on?" She skipped over to Alex's closet and started flipping through the hangers.

"Only my old football uniform," Alex said. "And something tells me you're not gonna want to wear that around the halls."

Alex gathered up the last of the popcorn and shoveled it in her mouth. It was about time to microwave their second batch.

"Speaking of football," Sophie said, "what are you going to do about sports in the spring?"

Alex took another deep breath and smiled. Having already had this conversation with her dad, she felt more comfortable this time telling Sophie her news.

"I'm thinking about trying out for soccer," she said, bracing herself for the response.

Sophie's eyes suddenly went wide. "Huh," she said. "Didn't see *that* coming."

"Honestly?" Alex said. "Neither did I."

"Spring soccer," Sophie said.

Alex nodded.

"The team you left to go play football? The one that flat-out rejected you because you were brave enough to chase your dreams?" Sophie said. "*That* girls' soccer team?"

"I'm trying to leave the past in the past," Alex said. "Kinda like beginning a new year. Starting fresh. New resolutions instead of old grudges." She grinned. "Not my grudges. Theirs."

"Uh-huh." Sophie nodded. "Well, I agree, holding grudges isn't healthy, but those girls were really awful to you," she said. "As a friend, I wouldn't want to see you go through that again."

Alex nodded at the empty bowl.

"Should we go make more?" she said to Sophie.

"*Not* until we finish this conversation," Sophie said. "Wasn't one of the reasons you went out for football because you didn't really love soccer? You said it wasn't your passion."

"It wasn't," Alex said. "And I never got the same feeling from soccer that I did from being a quarterback. But . . . I don't know. I miss it, I guess."

"What about Lindsey?" Sophie asked. "It would mean being on the same team with her again. And it's not as if you guys were pals even before the whole football thing happened."

"It's like you always say," Alex said. "Lindsey gonna Lindsey.

But I honestly don't think the other girls are mad at me anymore. The last couple of weeks before break they were being a lot nicer."

"Everybody gets nicer around Christmas!" Sophie proclaimed.

"Hey," Alex said, "whose side are you on?"

"Yours," Sophie said, with her hands up in defense. "Forever. But as much as I know you love competing and being on a team, I also know that you *hate* drama."

"But you have to admit I did create some," Alex said. "For the soccer team *and* the football team."

"Listen," Sophie said. "Whatever you decide, you know I've got your back. But it's New Year's Eve. So we don't have to decide this tonight, right?"

Alex remembered her dad saying something similar on Christmas Eve. She didn't have to make her decision now, but time was ticking. Like the countdown to a new year. She'd have to make up her mind someday.

"You know what they say," Alex said. "Ring out the old, ring in the new."

Sophie sighed.

"Yeah," she scoffed. "New *drama*."

They decided to FaceTime Gabe and Jabril, who were having a sleepover at Jabril's house tonight. Before long it became a party of four, all of them laughing and talking at once, her three best friends in the world.

Alex knew she wouldn't have made it through football without them. It made her appreciate having them in her life, and on her side, even more. Of course, when Alex mentioned wanting to play spring soccer, Gabe and Jabril were both on board.

"Alex Carlisle, king of all seventh-grade sports in Orville!" Gabe Hildreth said.

"Wouldn't it be 'queen'?" Sophie said.

"Whatever," Gabe said. "Point is, this girl is on fire!"

Sophie grinned. "Somebody ought to write a song like that," she said.

Somehow Alex and Sophie stayed awake until midnight, even though Alex could see her friend starting to fade with about a half hour to go. By then they'd gone through their third bowl of popcorn.

Finally, they counted down from ten, watching the sparkling crystal-studded ball begin to drop on the TV in Alex's room. Jack had given them two fancy champagne flutes, and Sophie filled them to the brim with sparkling cider. Right at midnight, they clinked their glasses together like they'd seen people do on television and toasted to the new year. Alex didn't know why, but it felt a little bit like her birthday, as if it were time to blow out the candles and make a wish.

Sophie fell asleep right away, but Alex was wide awake. Maybe from the fizziness of the cider. Or maybe because she had a lot on her mind.

She lay there with her head on her pillow, staring up at the ceiling, and thought again about how lucky she was to have people in her life who loved and cared about her. Thought about how grateful she was to have gotten the chance to play football, to show herself and the whole town that she wasn't just good enough to make the team, but to play starting quarterback in the championship game.

That was last season, though.

That was last *year*.

She wanted her next season, *this* year, to be about soccer again. At least in the spring.

Closing her eyes now, just a few minutes into the new year, she whispered, "Brave and bold" into the darkness, made a wish about her luck holding, and finally drifted off to sleep.

It was the same every year. You loved being off from school, then couldn't wait to get *back* to school.

Alex's first class on Monday morning was English, with Mrs. McQuade. It was Alex's favorite class, not just because it was all about reading and writing but because Mrs. McQuade made it fun.

Alex still hadn't made up her mind about soccer. But one thing she knew about herself was that she loved a challenge. It was all tied up with her desire to compete. And there was a part of her, a big part, that liked the idea that she could be a difference-maker. Someone who might tip the scales in the team's favor if they made it to the league championship again.

Lindsey Stiles was in Mrs. McQuade's class. So were Annie Burgess and Carly Jones, the goalkeeper for the girls' team, and Ally McGee, their star defender. Sophie was here too, along with Gabe and Jabril.

Once they were seated and the bell rang, Mrs. McQuade had everyone go around the room and talk about something fun they'd done over break.

When it was Alex's turn, she said, "The two best things I did were celebrate New Year's Eve with Sophie and watch football on TV with my dad."

From behind her she heard Lindsey Stiles mutter, "Do you wear your uniform and helmet when you watch?"

Lindsey laughed then. But no one else in the classroom did. Alex gave a quick look over to Sophie, who raised her eyebrows as high as they could go and silently mouthed one word:

Wow.

Maybe, Alex thought, the other soccer girls weren't following Lindsey's lead the way they had last fall.

"Let's face it, Linds," Gabe said from across the room. "The only time Alex needs a helmet when she's not playing football is when you're around."

At that, pretty much everyone in Mrs. McQuade's class erupted with laughter.

"Now, now," Mrs. McQuade said, trying to settle everyone down. "It's a new year, which means a good time for everybody to adjust their attitudes around each other in a positive way." She smiled. "At least when you're with me."

Mrs. McQuade wasted no time diving into the semester's curriculum. They were discussing their first reading assignment of the year, *Alice's Adventures in Wonderland* by Lewis Carroll. Alex was only halfway through, but it was already becoming one of her favorite books. Right up there with *The Princess Bride*. Her favorite line so far was "Sometimes I believe as many as six impossible things before breakfast."

It was a little like football, Alex thought. Only she'd never thought of making the team as impossible. More like the season had been her own version of Wonderland.

When class was over, Alex, Sophie, and Annie walked together toward history.

"Don't tell her I said this," Annie said. "But Lindsey has *got* to let this thing go."

Sophie snorted. "Like that's going to happen."

"She acts like I ruined your whole season," Alex said.

"And guess what?" Annie said. "When we got to the championship game, the other team was just better that day."

Annie hadn't just ended up being captain of the team but MVP too. When Alex was still playing, Annie had been the striker to her right. But when Annie moved over to play center middie, she played as if that had been her position all along. One of the things Alex had missed the most about soccer was playing alongside Annie. The two of them had made a great team, always anticipating each other's moves, ready to pass the ball if the other was in better position to score.

It was different with Lindsey, who'd played to Alex's left. When she ended up with the ball, whether she had open field in front of her or not, you rarely saw it again. Her one big idea was to carry the ball to the keeper herself, like she didn't believe in passing. Alex's dad had once said that in basketball they called players like Lindsey Stiles "ball stoppers."

Nobody ever said it to her face, but some of the other players called her "Lindsey Styles." She played as if a camera were following her every move.

There were still a few minutes before history, so they stopped outside the classroom.

Sophie turned to Alex. "So, are you gonna tell her or should I?"

"Tell me *what*?" Annie said, alternating looks between Alex and Sophie.

Alex lowered her voice.

"I was going to wait until after school to tell you," she said, "because your opinion matters to me. But I'm thinking I might want to come out for soccer."

Annie looked at Alex with a blank expression.

"But I thought you quit soccer," she said, somewhat puzzled.

"I never thought about it that way," Alex said. "I just wanted to try something different. And find out if I was good enough to play football. But there's no football in the spring."

Alex was studying Annie's face, trying to read it the way she would a book, attempting to predict what she thought about the matter.

"So you'd just be doing it to have something to do," Annie said, sounding a little hurt.

"No, no, no," Alex said. "Nothing like that. I just realized how much I missed playing with my friends." She grinned. "At least when they were still my friends."

"I'm your friend," Annie said.

"I know you are," Alex said. "More than anything, I missed playing alongside *you*."

There was a silence now that Alex thought was beyond awkward.

"So what do you think?" she said to Annie.

There was a slight hesitation before Annie smiled and said, "I think you should go for it!"

The bell rang then, and Alex followed Sophie and Annie into Mr. Frye's classroom, wondering if what she'd heard was fake enthusiasm from Annie and whether she really thought the idea was all that great.

And if someone as cool as Annie, somebody who'd stood up for Alex when none of the other soccer girls had, didn't want her on the team, then who would?

"WHAT IF WINNING OVER THE SOCCER GIRLS IS GOING TO BE JUST AS hard as winning over the football team?" Alex said to Gabe and Jabril at lunch.

Gabe and Jabril gave each other a knowing glance and smiled.

"That sound brave to you?" Jabril said.

Gabe shook his head. "Come to think of it, doesn't sound bold either."

Alex wrinkled her nose, teasingly elbowing Gabe in the side while kicking Jabril under the table. "I knew I shouldn't have told you two about my resolution," she said.

"First of all," said Jabril, "that resolution is meaningless because you already *are* those things. If you weren't, we wouldn't have those pictures of us posing with the championship trophy."

"Shame none of those pictures caught your good side," Gabe said to Jabril.

"Yeah, yeah, say what you want," Jabril said. "Just be glad that I was playing for *your* side."

Alex looked past Gabe and Jabril, a couple of tables over, and saw Lindsey sitting with the other girls from the soccer team. Now Lindsey looked up, staring daggers at Alex.

She knows, Alex thought.

"Don't turn around," Alex said, "but I am currently getting a death glare from Lindsey. No way she'll let this happen."

"Come *on*," Gabe said. "Lindsey won't have anything to say about it. It's not like she's captain, and anyway, only the coach gets to decide who makes the team."

"And," Jabril said, "from what I heard this morning, no one seems to be joining Lindsey's anti-Alex fan club. She's the only one still hanging on to this stupid vendetta."

Alex knew they were right, but a part of her still worried that Lindsey could convince the other girls to ice her out.

"You just gotta go for it," Gabe said. "Anybody who doesn't want you on that team doesn't really want to win, that's the way I look at it."

"I just miss *being* on the team," Alex admitted. "When my friends were still my friends. Now every time I watch the US women's soccer team kicking butt, I miss it even more."

"So you play," Gabe said, like it was simple. "Even if J and I will be on the sidelines this time instead of on the field with you."

"Done deal," Jabril said.

"You guys make it sound so easy," Alex said.

"Is anything worth doing ever easy?" said Gabe.

She had to admit, he had a point.

And while they might not be on the football field any longer, they were still very much a team.

THEY'D BEEN BACK AT SCHOOL FOR A FEW WEEKS NOW, BUT THE actual start to spring soccer season was a long way off, not until the first week of March. They weren't even holding tryouts until February, after which the girls would practice in the gymnasium until the weather was decent enough for them to go outside. In other words, not ten below zero.

After the last bell of the day, and before Alex got on the bus home, Sophie and Alex walked past the gym and saw the huge corkboard outside the double doors announcing the tryout dates for all the spring sports. There was a sign-up sheet pinned up for each one.

It's not as if I don't have other options besides soccer, Alex told herself as she stood in front of the board.

Sophie was already dressed in her cheerleading uniform, getting ready for the seventh-grade boys' basketball game in half an hour. She sipped a bottle of red Gatorade while Alex pored over the corkboard, checking out her options.

"You're staring at that board like it's a crystal ball, about to determine your future," Sophie said.

"I'm thinking maybe I don't need to play soccer," Alex said, her eyes scanning over the flyer for spring track.

"Nobody said you *needed* to," Sophie said. "I just thought you wanted to."

"I do," Alex said. "Or at least I thought I did before I got that sketchy vibe off Annie. And she's supposed to be my biggest advocate."

"Annie's fine," Sophie said, waving Alex off. "Probably just surprised you wanted to rejoin the team is all."

"But say the coach wants to put me back at center middie," Alex said. "How would Annie feel about that?"

"And how many things are we going to worry about today?" Sophie said.

Alex ignored her and pointed at the board.

"What about tennis?" she said. "I could totally see myself playing tennis!"

"You've never even picked up a racket!" Sophie said.

"Hadn't played football either."

Sophie gave Alex a look as if to say, *Those two sports could not be more different, and you know it.*

"Even so," Sophie said. "They're going to have the same six players they had last year. The only person they'd probably make room for is Serena."

"What about track?" Alex said. "You're the one always telling me how fast I am."

"I know they call it a track *team*," Sophie said. "But in the end, even if you're running a relay, it's still just you against the clock. Alone."

Alex looked away from the board now and turned to Sophie. "And how is this helping me?" she asked.

"I'm *helping* you," Sophie said, "by telling you to play soccer." She smiled. "The world's most popular sport."

"Yeah," Alex said. "With the school's most *un*popular ex-soccer player."

One of Sophie's teammates came running down the hallway then, and Sophie glanced at her watch. "To be continued," she said, twisting the cap on her drink and grabbing her duffel bag.

She patted Alex on the shoulder, then headed inside the gym to start warming up with her team.

With Sophie gone, Alex drew her attention to the only thing on the board that mattered: the sign-up sheet for soccer. A couple of her classmates who hadn't made the team last fall had already written their names in, even though there was a message at the top of the sheet that read:

THIS TEAM WILL ONLY BE ABLE TO TAKE ON
A FEW NEW PLAYERS.

IF YOU PLAYED ON THE TEAM DURING THE FALL
SEASON, YOU ARE AUTOMATICALLY ON THE ROSTER.
ALL OTHERS MUST PARTICIPATE IN TRYOUTS TO BE
CONSIDERED FOR THE TEAM THIS SPRING.

It almost read to Alex like a warning. And although she'd played spring soccer in the sixth grade, and everybody in school knew she would have made the fall team, she wasn't exactly sure where she stood now.

"You're not technically part of the team. You get that, right?"

She didn't even have to turn around to know who the voice was coming from. It was unmistakable.

Lindsey.

When you shadowed a player in soccer, it was called ghosting. They'd only been back at school for a few weeks, and already Alex felt as if she were being ghosted by Lindsey Stiles.

Alex sighed and turned around, forcing a smile, even though both of them knew it was phony.

"I can read," she said.

She was starting to think she should have expanded her resolution. *Be bold. Be brave. Beware of seventh graders named Lindsey Stiles.*

"Just wanted to make sure you didn't miss the fine print about the rules," Lindsey said.

"*Fine?*" Alex said. "If the print about us adding new players were any bigger—"

"*Us?*" Lindsey interrupted. "Allow me to fill you in—this team stopped being *yours* when you decided to play football last season."

"You know that's not what I meant."

"Did you really tell Annie that you missed us?" Lindsey said, doing her best to embarrass Alex.

"Did Annie volunteer that?" Alex said.

"I saw you two talking in the hall and I asked her," Lindsey said. "So if that's the case, how come you didn't worry about missing us last fall?"

"I did," Alex said, trying to keep an even tone, "whether you believe it or not."

"You quit," Lindsey said.

"Because I wanted to find out if I was good enough to play

football," Alex said. "I wanted to try something new."

"Here's an idea," Lindsey said. "Try something new in the spring."

Then she turned and walked away.

Yay, team, Alex thought. And headed for the bus.

7

ALEX WAS HAPPY TO BE BACK AT SCHOOL. SHE LIKED TO BE BUSY AND had never been afraid of a little work. Even a lot of work. She liked challenging herself. To her, it was just another way of competing.

She liked winning, of course. There was no getting around that. But to Alex, competing was about more than just keeping score. It was about achieving her best.

Over the next few weeks, she tried keeping herself distracted with homework and studying so she wouldn't obsess about spring soccer. After discussing it with Sophie and Gabe and Jabril, by now she was all talked out.

And anyway, talking wasn't going to win her a spot on the team. That is, when and if she decided to try out.

The subject came up again at dinner the following evening, despite Alex trying to avoid it altogether. Though they were almost to February now, and her dad would want to know what she'd decided.

"Still thinking about it," she said when he'd asked her the inevitable.

"Sounded to me all the way back on Christmas Eve as if you'd *already* thought about it," he said.

Alex let out a long breath. "It's just—" She paused, composing herself. "What if I don't make it?"

Her dad looked up from his chicken cutlet and set his fork down on the plate. "I know that's not my daughter talking," he said.

He smiled at her.

"Want to kick it around a little more?" he said, winking.

"Good one, Dad," she said. "But I really have kicked it around enough, with you and all my friends. I just have to figure it out myself."

"You always do," he said.

After dinner, she went upstairs to her room, pressed play on Taylor Swift's newest album, then plopped down on her bed and closed her eyes.

What if she wasn't the same soccer player she'd been last year? She was completely out of practice. Sure, football and soccer required some of the same skills—running, strategy, looking up the field for open teammates. But Alex had to admit she might be a little rusty.

Which called something else into question. What if the girls trying out—the ones who hadn't made the team last fall—had been training in their off time, improving their skills? They might even be better than Alex now.

But that wasn't the biggest question of all, and Alex knew it. Because the biggest question of all was this:

If the other girls on the team wouldn't accept her, did she really want to be on a team with *them*? She knew what it was like to be shunned by those girls.

As much as she wanted to play, did she really want to go through all that again?

Her dad said she always figured things out, but Alex wasn't so sure this time. She closed her eyes and listened to the music and wondered if Taylor Swift had had this much trouble figuring out seventh grade.

For now, though, she knew she was on her own.

Again.

When Alex got home from school the next day, she knew exactly what she needed to do:

She needed to *move*.

So she put on her black-and-gold Steelers hoodie, found her soccer cleats underneath the piles of sneakers and shoes in her closet, and tried them on to see if they still fit. They were a little snug, but they would do for now, Alex thought, as she headed down to the garage and grabbed her Adidas ball. Clutching it under her arm against her hip, she rounded the corner of the house outside and into the backyard.

The snow had almost completely melted, and the sun was out. It was cold, but not too cold. And once Alex started moving, started working up a sweat, she felt good. Really good. She felt the warmth of the sun on her face and imagined it was already spring. That tryouts were over and she'd made the team.

She pushed the ball up and down the yard, pretending it was open field in front of her, left foot, right foot, left foot, occasionally making a pass to an imaginary teammate, using a tree or fence post as a target.

Alex's cheeks were flushed, and a little frozen from the cold, but she smiled all the same.

The simplest things in sports could make you happy, if you could just get out of your own way.

It made her feel like herself again. Alex wasn't a worrier by nature. She'd sometimes doubt herself in sports, like she did at the start of football season. When it felt as if she were competing against her own team. But the feeling didn't last long.

She ran faster now, pushing the ball without ever having to look down, picking it up occasionally and tossing it in the air so she could practice using her chest or head to direct it, controlling the ball the way she used to. It was funny, she thought: one of the things she'd told herself last fall was that she'd never be great at soccer.

But soccer was making her feel pretty great right now.

She had originally only planned to spend a half hour out here at most. But she was having too much fun. The first thirty minutes were more like a warm-up.

She ran back to the garage, and after rummaging past a few shovels and gardening tools, she pulled out the small soccer goal her dad had bought her last year. Dragging it out back, she set it up near the tree line, so she'd have the slight wind at her back.

She took shots from all angles, getting in some practice with both feet. She was naturally right-footed but had always been able to kick with either one. They called you "two-footed" in soccer when you could do that. The goal may have been three-quarters as wide as a normal soccer goal, but before long she was hitting it with ease, low to the corners, high to the corners. Left foot. Right foot.

Really feeling it now.

She set the ball down in front of her and backed away a few paces, pretending she was about to take a penalty kick during overtime to win the big game.

She inhaled deeply, picking her spot against the imaginary keeper, then took a running start and—

Score. She buried the ball with her left foot into the upper right-hand corner of the net.

Setting the ball down again, she used her right foot this time, stepping into the kick and sending the ball rolling across the grass into the left corner of the goal.

Out here, alone, she felt like an athlete. It was fun to talk about sports—player stats, margins, hypothetical situations. Her dad said that any conversation about sports, didn't matter which, was part of the fun of being a fan.

Not as much fun, Alex thought, as being on the field, or the court, or wherever else sports happened.

When she took a break, she looked up and saw her dad watching from his office on the second floor. He waved. She waved back. Then he opened the window.

"I can't decide," he called down to her, "whether you remind me more of Megan Rapinoe or Alex Morgan."

"Ha!" she yelled back. "But if you have a choice, I say you always go with an Alex."

It was getting close to dinnertime when she put away her equipment and came inside to take a shower. She had just begun on homework when the doorbell rang.

Maybe it was a package, Alex thought. Sometimes the mail

carriers didn't make it to their house until late in the evening.

"I got it," her dad said, clambering down the stairs. "Time for me to pay off on your IOU."

"My IOU?" Alex asked.

"How quickly they forget," he said.

Then Alex remembered. Christmas Eve. The certificate. The mysterious way her dad presented the gift. Alex had to admit, curiosity was getting the better of her.

She jerked up from her desk chair and followed her dad downstairs.

He was waiting to open the door, hand on the knob, beaming back at Alex.

"What's going on—"

But before she could finish her sentence, the door swung open.

Standing on the other side, in the light of the porch lamp, was someone she never expected to see.

ALEX NEARLY KNOCKED HER DAD OVER AS SHE BLEW BY HIM AND jumped into her mother's arms.

"Merry Christmas," Dr. Liza Borelli whispered into her ear.

Alex gripped her mom tight around the waist. "Didn't Christmas already come and go?" she asked, her voice muffled into her mom's wool coat.

"Oh, you know stuff always arrives late this time of year," her mom joked as Alex finally pulled back.

"Hey, you," Jack said to Alex's mom, pulling her in for a side hug.

She smiled at him. "Hey yourself. I was sure you'd cave and tell her."

"It was strictly the fear of what you might do to me if I spoiled your surprise," he said.

The best thing about their divorce, Alex knew, was that they had remained good friends. They still loved each other, just not the way they once had. Alex understood not every child of divorced parents had it so well. She might not get to see her mom all that often, but she had two loving, supportive parents. And that was all she needed.

A few minutes later they were all in the living room, Alex seated next to her mom on the couch, Jack on the recliner across from them.

"Okay," Alex said. "Spill. What are you doing here?"

Liza had a big job as a surgeon in a major hospital in San Francisco and rarely got time off. In fact, on many occasions, she'd have to hang up early on her calls with Alex because of an emergency or to check on a patient. So though Alex was excited to see her mother, she was aware it was nothing short of a miracle she was here at all.

"I didn't want to tell you until I was absolutely certain it was going to happen," her mom said.

"Tell me what?" Alex said.

Liza looked across the room at her ex-husband, the two seeming to share some kind of inside knowledge. It was driving Alex mad.

"Tell me *what*?" Alex repeated, getting antsy. Even though she knew it had to be good news.

"I'm moving back to the area for a few months," her mom said, "to give a series of lectures at the Pittsburgh Children's Hospital."

Alex's heart sped up in her chest. This was not the surprise she was expecting, and yet it was everything she could ever hope for and more.

"No *way*!" Alex yelled.

"Way," her mom said.

"What about Richard and Connor?" Alex asked.

Richard was her mom's new husband. Alex still thought of him that way, even though he wasn't exactly new any longer. They'd been married for seven years, and he was a doctor at the same hospital as her mom, a specialist in sports medicine. They'd met during their residency. Connor was their five-year-old son,

Alex's half brother, even though she'd only met him once, the time she flew to San Francisco.

"They'll probably come to visit one time while I'm here," she said. "And I'll fly back *Out There* a couple of times."

It was how she referred to San Francisco. *Out There.* She sometimes made it sound like another planet. And to Alex, it almost was.

"It'll be rough being separated from them," her mom continued. "But this was such a great honor, with a wonderful hospital. I couldn't pass up the chance to help educate other medical professionals about my specialty."

Her specialty was pediatric surgery.

"So what I've done is rented a small apartment next to the hospital, because they've asked me to see patients while I'm in residence," she said. "It would have been a bit too much of a commute every day if I'd gotten a place here. And I figured if the Steelers aren't too far away, neither is your old mom."

"Are you *kidding*?" Alex said. "I'm going to get to see you, like, all the time!"

Her mom gave her a warm smile and leaned over to kiss the side of her head.

"Okay," Alex said, turning to her dad. "Now this really is the best Christmas ever."

"Just call me Santa Claus," he said.

Jack had a special dinner planned for Alex's mom's arrival: grilled lamb chops. He was already on his way outside to throw down the charcoal and fire up the grill.

"How can I help?" Liza said once they were in the kitchen.

"Salad," Jack called over his shoulder, as he opened the sliding glass door to the patio.

"Hey," Alex said, "salads are usually my job when you grill."

"Work it out with the doc," he said.

A half hour later they were sitting at the kitchen table. The three of them. Alex and her parents. Alex couldn't remember the last time they'd done this. When her mom had surprised her by showing up for Alex's football championship game, they'd gone out to dinner once before she flew back to San Francisco the next morning.

This was different. Just knowing they'd have the chance to do this more often in the next few months sent a pleasant warmth into Alex's chest. The longest Alex had ever spent with her mom since the divorce had been a week. She was so excited by the prospect of having her mom present in her life for this long. It was as if Christmas had been extended this year.

Suddenly the whole idea of soccer had shrunk down small enough to fit inside the palm of her hand. Her mom was here. *Right* here. And she didn't have to fly back to the West Coast tomorrow either. She was *living* here. Into the spring.

"Hey," her mom said now. "Where did your mind just wander off to?"

"I was just wondering if I was dreaming," Alex said.

When they'd finished dinner and cleaned up the kitchen, Alex's mom said she needed a post-meal walk, especially after the s'mores Alex's dad had assembled for the special occasion.

Jack told them to go ahead without him, he had some work

upstairs he still needed to finish up. Alex's mom grabbed her coat, Alex put on her hoodie and puffer jacket, and out they went for a walk around the neighborhood. Or what Alex's dad liked to call "securing the perimeter."

It had gotten a few degrees colder after the sun had gone down. But not too cold for a walk with her mom. They had been talking more on the phone over the past few months. But this wasn't FaceTime.

This was actual MomTime.

"So how's my girl?" Liza said, knocking her hip into Alex as they walked.

"I'm good," Alex said. "Still kind of coming down off everything that happened in football. It's only been a few months, but every time I look back, it's like it happened to somebody else."

"It didn't happen to somebody else," Liza said. "It happened to you, honey. And what's more, you made something happen in this town that they'll be talking about forever."

"I don't know about *forever*," Alex said, feeling a bit awkward. She never looked at herself that way. As someone who'd be remembered.

"You should give yourself more credit," her mom said. "You sent all the girls in this town a powerful message about the way things ought to be for *all* girls."

"There were a bunch of times when I didn't think I was going to make it," Alex admitted.

"Hey," her mom said, "there were plenty of times I didn't think I was going to get into medical school. Let alone make it *through* medical school."

"And now look at you," Alex said, "a big fancy-pants lecturer at one of the most famous hospitals in the whole country."

They had no destination. Weren't in any hurry. They strolled up Miller Road, took a left on Running Brook, then a right onto Jonah's Path. Alex had often wondered what it would be like to have more mother-daughter chats like this in person. Now they were doing it. It was the first of many, Alex was sure. *Merry Christmas to me,* she thought.

"So," her mom said, "are we going to talk about soccer before we make it all the way to Murrayville?"

"Dad told," Alex said, not that it surprised her.

"Only after you said you were done talking about it with him."

"And figured I could make an exception for my old mom . . ."

Alex's mom pinched her lightly on the arm. "Who you calling *old?*"

Alex took her through all of it. From the beginning. Her mom already knew some of the details, like Lindsey Stiles giving her grief for quitting soccer. But Alex updated her on the new developments. Like Annie's reaction when Alex told her she might try out for soccer in the spring.

"I don't want to feel like an outsider on my own team," Alex said. "Been there, done that."

"You won't," her mom said.

Like it was a known fact. Her mom had always admitted she didn't know a ton about sports. Especially football. She'd been a cross-country runner in high school and still ran forty miles a week. Recently she'd even competed in a few five-kilometer races on the West Coast.

"You don't know that, Mom," Alex said. "No offense, but it's been a while since you were twelve."

They stopped under a streetlight, and Liza laid a hand on her daughter's shoulder.

"Let me explain something that you'll understand a lot better when you are as old as me," she said. "That twelve-year-old kid never leaves any of us."

They turned back toward home. Alex looked up at the sky. There was a huge moon tonight, lighting Orville, Pennsylvania, along with the stars.

"What do you think I should do?" Alex said, genuinely wanting her mom's opinion. She often gave solid advice for tough situations like this one.

"You play," she said. "One hundred percent. You play your little butt off. And anybody who doesn't want you as a teammate ought to think about going bowling instead."

Alex had a gut feeling her mom would say that. Liza never shied away from a challenge. One day, Alex hoped to be half as brave as her mom.

"If I do join the team," Alex said, "I'd want to tell the coach I don't need to play my old position."

"Center middie."

Alex was equal parts shocked and delighted her mom remembered the name.

"It's Annie's position now, and she was great last fall," Alex said. "I wanted QB when I went out for football. But it really doesn't matter where I play in soccer."

"You should probably leave that up to the coach," her mom said. "Who *is* the coach, by the way?"

"Our other coach took a job in Philadelphia," Alex said. "The new coach is some woman named Mrs. Cross?"

"Mrs. Cross as in Hannah Cross?"

Alex shrugged. "I think so," she said. "Why, who's Hannah Cross?"

"Only the greatest player in the history of Orville High," Liza said. "She was there when I was."

"I heard she just moved back here with her husband and their son," Alex said.

"Oh, honey, how great will it be playing for Hannah Cross?" her mom said, almost starry-eyed.

They were back at the house by now, on their way up the front walk.

Before heading back inside, Liza took Alex's hand in hers.

"You go for this, Alex," she said in earnest. "Whether Lindsey Stiles or anyone else says they don't want you on the team. They don't make the rules. They don't get to decide. You didn't let the jerks on the football team run you off. You're certainly not going to let a few naysayers get in your way now."

Alex's lips perked up into a smile, and her mom squeezed her hand tight.

"I don't mean to get preachy . . ." she said.

"Not you, Mom," Alex said, grinning back. "Never."

"Very funny," she said. "But seriously? After what you went through last fall, you're *way* past letting somebody define your role."

"If you had," Alex said, "you wouldn't be a doctor and you wouldn't be here."

"Bingo," her mom said.

"It's funny how things change," Alex said as they hung up their coats in the front closet. "I left soccer because football was my dream. Now here I am, eager to get back to playing soccer."

Her mom wrapped an arm around Alex right then.

"That's the thing about dreams," she said. "They don't just come one to a customer."

Her mom made it sound so simple.

It wasn't.

10

ALEX'S MOM CAME OVER EVERY DAY THAT WEEKEND. THEY WENT out to dinner on Saturday night, just the two of them. Then, Sunday afternoon, Alex brought her mom into their backyard and they kicked the soccer ball around together.

"I'm going to turn you into a player," Alex said.

"You wouldn't dare," her mom said, laughing.

Alex passed her the ball, and her mom stopped it with her foot. "If you can run," Alex said, "you can play soccer."

"There's running," her mom said, "and there's kicking a ball *while* running."

"C'mon," Alex said. "It'll be fun."

"What's next, you teach me how to be a football catcher?"

Alex sighed and shook her head. "They're called wide receivers, Mom."

Alex demonstrated a few moves, showing her mom how to control the ball with the sides of her feet, how to plant and swing her leg when taking a shot. And before long, Liza started to get the hang of it. It even turned out that she could kick with both feet. When Alex explained how useful that was in soccer, and how she could do it too, her mom pumped both fists in the air.

"I knew you inherited something from me!" she said.

"A lot more than kicking a soccer ball, I hope."

Finally, just for fun, Alex put her mom in the goal, showing her how to get into position, weight balanced equally on both feet so you could set up to move in either direction. Arms relaxed at the sides.

Alex wasn't kicking the ball as hard as she normally would. That would be unfair. But after a while, her mom was getting pretty good at making stops.

"Is there a position open for me on the team?" she said after tipping one of Alex's shots over the crossbar.

"Ha!" Alex said. "I'm going easy on you."

"Time to dial it up," her mom said. "Find out what I'm capable of."

"You sure?"

"Bring it, kid."

Alex used a move she'd been working on recently. It started out like any other kick, winding up for a big shot. Then, at the last moment, once you had the keeper leaning, you practically froze the frame and pushed it into the net with the opposite foot.

She did that now. *Huge* windup, like she was aiming to kick the ball all the way into the woods behind their house. Her mom was watching closely, so she really had to sell it. Then she came to an abrupt stop, switching feet and kicking the ball with her left foot into the corner to her mom's right, just as her mom was leaning in the other direction.

When Liza tried to adjust, she ended up sitting on the ground, looking like she'd just experienced whiplash.

"Oops," she said.

They both laughed their heads off, like a couple of

twelve-year-olds. Maybe her mom was right. Maybe the little kid in you never really left.

Soccer tryouts were scheduled for the following Wednesday after school. Mrs. Cross had moved them up when she heard they were predicting an unusually warm week for this time of year.

After being around her mom and having the Big Talk about soccer that first night, Alex knew she couldn't *not* go out for the team. That Monday she'd gotten to school early, made a beeline for the corkboard outside the gym, and printed her name on the tryout sheet.

It felt good. Empowering. To see her name up there in black and white. It was a small gesture, but symbolic of a decision that'd been hanging over her head for weeks.

The next few days dragged by painfully slowly. Now that Alex had made up her mind, all she wanted was to get out there and get after it.

So when Wednesday rolled around, Alex was ready.

She'd packed a duffel that morning—cleats, shin guards, socks, and a sweatband—and stored it in her locker until the final bell rang.

The soccer hopefuls were to gather in the gym on the bleachers closest to the double doors at four o'clock sharp.

Alex noticed about twelve other girls sitting with her in the stands, none of whom she recognized. For all she knew, they could all be star players. The thought made Alex sweat, and she wiped a hand through her hair.

After about five minutes, a short woman who must have been

Mrs. Cross came though the gym doors carrying a mesh bag full of soccer balls over one shoulder.

She wore her short blonde hair in a tight ponytail and wore track pants with a T-shirt over a long-sleeved shirt. A whistle hung low around her neck.

Setting the bag down, she grabbed a loose ball that'd rolled out and started bouncing it off her feet and knees and chest, never letting it touch the ground, like some kind of soccer magician. Alex thought, *She must have been something to see when she played for Orville High.*

Gabe and Jabril said you could always tell if somebody was a "baller."

Hannah Cross was no doubt one.

She kicked the ball down the court and ran to catch up with it, skidding to a halt right in front of the girls.

Introducing herself briefly, she talked fast. Cutting right to the chase and explaining how tryouts would be organized.

The tryouts would be an abridged version of those in the fall, Coach Cross explained. One two-hour session to evaluate their skills, in order to fill three open spots on the team. One of last season's starters, Liz Duffy, had moved to Oregon with her family in December. Two other starters had decided to try lacrosse.

"I'm going to put you through as many drills as we have time for," Coach Cross said. "And I'll make sure to give each of you the opportunity to show off your agility and ball skills, because I'm sure you all have them. As much as I wish there were more open spots on the team, there just aren't."

Then she clapped her hands and said, "Let's have some fun!"

She led them outside onto the soccer field and divided them into two groups of six.

First she had everyone stand about thirty feet across from each other and kick the ball back and forth as a warm-up and to—as she put it—get a feel for the ball. Alex was paired with Roisin Wright, a transfer student from Ireland who, Alex could tell right away, was a baller herself.

They were in some classes together, and Alex had grown to really like her. She also loved her name, which was pronounced *Ro-sheen*.

When they stopped for a quick water break, Roisin said to Alex, "You're good, I can tell."

"Not as good as you!" Alex said, but she was flattered by the compliment nonetheless.

"Ah," Roisin said in her lilting accent, "anybody can git themselves lookin' good."

Alex giggled, but she could tell Roisin was just being modest. It was clear to anyone that Roisin had mad skills.

The next drill included various dribbling exercises. First dribbling a ball up and down the field by yourself, then pairing up. After that they practiced throw-ins, and Coach Cross explained that throw-ins might be one of the most underappreciated skills in soccer, because a good, quick, hard throw-in after a change of possession could be as important as a pass with your feet.

"And," she said, "if you're not the goalie, it's the only time you get to use your hands!"

At the next water break Coach Cross came over to Alex on the sidelines.

"You're the quarterback, right?" she said.

Alex smiled. "Well," she said, "I think Patrick Mahomes is *the* quarterback. I just played for the Owls last season."

"From what I heard, you did a lot more than that," Coach Cross said before running back onto the field, blowing her whistle to get everyone's attention.

Alex didn't know how to feel about the coach's comment. On the one hand, it was nice to hear that she was noticed for her achievements. On the other, it was like an invisible weight had settled over her shoulders. As if she were carrying the responsibility of gender equality for all the girls in the town. It was both humbling and stressful.

Coach Cross announced that they'd be moving on to scoring drills. As they did, Alex noticed that some of the fall season girls were standing by the fence bordering the soccer field. Lindsey was there. So were Annie and Ally McGee.

Roisin poked Alex with an elbow and nodded in their direction.

"I was talkin' to Lindsey 'bout tryin' out," she said. "Wasn't aware that she practically invented soccer."

"Hear you," Alex said. "Pretty sure when she looks in the mirror, she sees Carli Lloyd looking back at her."

Carli Lloyd—maybe the greatest female US player of them all.

"Lookin' in the mirror, I'm thinkin'," Roisin said, "is something Lindsey does a lot."

When they were back on the field, doing three-on-two drills, Alex felt a sudden pang in her chest, similar to the one she had during football tryouts: all eyes on her, all over again.

This time it was different.

When she'd tried out for football, she thought she *might* be good enough to play quarterback.

Today, she *knew* she could play soccer. Not that she'd ever considered herself the star of the team or anything. Even though center middie was a star position. In fact, she'd always thought that Annie had a better all-around game. Carly was great as keeper. And Alex never saw a better defender in their league than Ally McGee. If she'd had to pin down her top skill as a soccer player, it was this:

She made everybody around her better.

And now here she was. Out here again, doing her best to show Coach Cross what she could do. With every drill and each exercise, Alex was reminded of just how much of a team sport soccer was. Everybody involved. Everybody getting to touch the ball. Everybody in constant motion. And that feeling, when the game was over, after your team had won, of knowing each player had done something to make it happen.

There was a reason, Alex thought, why people all over the world called it the most beautiful game.

When there were fifteen minutes left, Coach Cross had them split up six-on-six for a brief scrimmage. She told them to pretend they were playing extra time in a World Cup game. If one team was ahead at the end, the scrimmage was over. If they tied, they'd decide the winner with penalty kicks. One per side.

"Just three rules," Coach Cross said. "If you're open, shoot. If your teammate has a better position, pass it, and let her take the shot. Number three is most important: have fun."

Rashida Wallace, who was trying out for keeper, was on Alex

and Roisin's team. Georgia Garcia played keeper for the opposing side. She was also going out for backup keeper to Carly.

Alex was glad Coach chose to put Roisin at center and Alex to her right. She didn't want Annie thinking Alex was going out for her spot, especially with her watching from the fence.

Alicia Caulfield, maybe the fastest girl on the field today, was on Roisin's left.

The scrimmage was a blast. It was as if Roisin and Alex had been playing together all their lives. The other team scored the first two goals. But then Alex scored on a pass from Roisin, right before Alex returned the favor with a sweet left-footed pass to Roisin, who swiftly put the ball behind Georgia in the net.

The scrimmage was tied at 2–2 when Coach blew her whistle and announced it was time for the penalty kicks. The other team selected Afafa Agbayong to take the kick for their side. She'd proven during tryouts that she was among the stronger players on the field today.

Afafa drove toward the ball, pulling her leg back and letting loose, sending the ball low to Rashida's left. Rashida made an impressive dive and knocked the ball away.

Alex and Roisin's team now.

Coach looked over and said, "Okay, who's gonna take it?"

Alex pointed at Roisin. Roisin pointed at Alex. Everyone was giggling, except Alex didn't realize what they were laughing at until she turned around. The other four players on their team were also pointing toward her.

"Looks like you're up, Miss Carlisle," Coach said. "The only dissenting vote appears to be your own."

Georgia was in the goal now. Coach set the ball. It might not have been the exact ten-yard distance for a PK, but close enough.

As Alex walked out toward the ball, she glanced down to the other end of the field and saw what appeared to be the entire seventh-grade girls' team watching her.

Yeah, Alex thought, *I'm up.*

She reached for the ball, picked it up, and spun it, so that the Adidas logo was facing out. Not for any good reason. Just buying herself a little extra time. *It's just a tryout scrimmage*, she said to herself. *Don't overhype it.* But with everyone watching, it was still a moment, at least for her. She told herself it was the same as always: visualize yourself doing it, then execute.

She stood there, remembering when she and her mom were out in the backyard messing around. The kick Alex made that left her mom butt-down in the grass in front of the goal. The two of them laughing hysterically. But most importantly, the kick that started it all . . .

Alex's confidence was restored once she'd figured out exactly what she wanted to do.

The goal she'd scored against Georgia earlier had been a right-footer, high over Georgia's left shoulder. Georgia had no chance at blocking it. She was at a different angle now, but it didn't matter.

Coach blew the whistle.

Alex nodded at Georgia.

Georgia nodded at her.

Alex took a deep breath.

Then she took a few paces back and to her left, inhaling deeply before approaching the ball.

She hesitated just slightly as she swung her right leg back, making it look as though she was planning a repeat of her previous goal against Georgia.

Georgia leaned left, ready to dive.

At the last possible moment, Alex squared her shoulders, stepping down on her right foot, and pushed the ball with her left into the wide-open net.

Inside her head, she could almost hear her mom shouting, *"Goal!"*

Even Georgia nodded good-naturedly from the goal, appreciating the skill it had taken to fake her out that way.

Alex's teammates cheered and crowded around, clapping her on the back and congratulating her on the win. It wasn't until the noise subsided and everyone started heading for the locker room that Alex heard slow clapping coming from the fence near the field.

Lindsey.

"Can't win 'em all," Alex said to Roisin.

"Sometimes," Roisin said, "that girl is about as useful as a chocolate teapot."

Alex laughed, and then Roisin was laughing along with her before they noticed that Lindsey was the last girl on the team still watching. She glared at them before shouldering her backpack and turning toward the late buses.

But nothing, not even Lindsey Stiles's bad attitude, could bring Alex down.

11

Coach Cross said that the official girls' soccer roster would be posted on the corkboard outside the gym the following Monday.

Needless to say, for Alex, the wait was agonizing. But Coach Cross said she needed the time to carefully weigh the options. Everyone performed especially well during tryouts, and she owed it to the team not to make any hasty decisions.

The days passed slower than a Zamboni machine polishing ice.

Alex had school and homework and studying, of course, but her mind was 98 percent composed of soccer. Not even a hot chocolate with Sophie at the café in town could take her mind off the subject.

"You're worrying about nothing, you know," Sophie said at their table in the corner.

Alex had made it to Saturday. Just two more days until she'd have the answer to her biggest question. Her dad had let her ride her bike into town for a few hours to take her mind off things.

Except her mind was right back on that *one* thing.

"Am I?" Alex said. "Those girls were all pretty good out there."

Sophie took a sip from her mug. "Yeah, but don't forget," she said, "you made the winning goal. Coach Cross won't forget that easily."

Alex shrugged. "Maybe you're right, but—"

"No *buts*!" Sophie cut in. "Think positive. Think like a cheerleader!"

Alex laughed. "As long as I don't have to *move* like a cheerleader, I think I can handle that."

"Mmm," Sophie said, swallowing a mouthful of hot chocolate. "Speaking of—guess who's helping choreograph our qualifying routine for nationals?"

"No!" Alex said. "For real?"

Sophie beamed, nodding. "I'm supposed to present some of my ideas to the coaches at practice on Monday."

"Soph!" Alex cried, "That's amazing!"

Sophie shrugged it off like it was nothing, but Alex knew it was a big deal. Not just for Sophie but for any kid hoping to prove themselves.

"Looks like we both have big things to look forward to on Monday," she said, winking at Alex.

The two lifted their mugs and clinked them together, just like they had with their sparkling cider on New Year's.

They were toasting to new beginnings. To new opportunities. And most of all, to friendship.

On Monday, Alex could barely pay attention in any of her classes. Her brain was so distracted by the soccer list, she had trouble concentrating. Between each class, she raced to the corkboard to see if the roster had gone up, but every time she was disappointed. Coach Cross was probably waiting to post it until the end of the day, Alex thought.

When the final bell rang, Alex tried to stay calm. She even stopped by her locker first to put away a few books and grab her coat before heading toward the gym.

By the time she got there, though, a crowd had already begun to form. Among the crowd were Jabril, Gabe, Sophie, Roisin, a couple of other girls from tryouts, and the one and only Lindsey Stiles.

"It's about time!" Jabril said, a smile across his face.

"Looks like we'll be seeing a bit more of each other, eh, Alex?" Roisin said.

Alex jogged toward the board.

The sheet of paper with the roster was hanging by a red thumbtack.

Alex read through the names. Up top were the girls who'd played on the fall team.

Underneath, the headline read NEW PLAYERS, and below that, three names were listed.

One of them was Alex's.

The other two belonged to Roisin and Rashida.

"You ready for this, QB?" Gabe said, laying a hand on her shoulder.

Before she could respond, though, Lindsey chimed in, "Yeah. What exactly are you, Alex? A football player or a soccer player?"

Jabril spoke up then. "Didn't realize you could only be one thing," he said. "Pretty sure Michael Jordan played both basketball and baseball and no one seemed to mind."

Lindsey didn't have an immediate answer for that. Her brows

drew inward, and she brushed past Alex down the hall. "See you at practice," she said as she left.

Gabe rolled his eyes. Sophie just shook her head. But Alex smiled. So did Roisin.

They'd made it, and nothing was going to stop them now.

Not even Lindsey Stiles.

12

THEIR FIRST OFFICIAL PRACTICE WAS SUPPOSED TO BE AFTER SCHOOL on Thursday.

As always, the last class of the day ended at three. Practice at four. As soon as the bell rung, and with an hour before they'd all be meeting in the gym, Alex made a stop at the school library. It was her favorite place at Orville Middle. She liked to find her own private corner and read there, getting lost in the books. Adventure-filled fantasies and fascinating biographies. It was nice to escape, even for a few minutes.

When she got there, she walked to a far corner of the big front room, sat herself down on the floor against the shelves, and pulled out *Alice's Adventures in Wonderland* from her backpack. She hadn't decided how many pages she was going to read before practice, though she was determined not to go too fast. That was the trouble with a really good book. Sometimes you had to force yourself to stop so you could enjoy it for longer. Savor every page.

But Alex let herself go this time, flipping pages to find out what would happen next.

Without realizing how much time had passed, she looked up suddenly and saw Annie Burgess standing over her, face red, out of breath, eyes on fire.

"I've been looking all over school for you!" Annie said.

Alex quickly checked her phone. It was only three thirty. What was Annie all worked up about?

Alex made a motion with her hands for Annie to keep her voice down. "Library," she whispered.

Annie sat down next to Alex, almost collapsing onto the floor.

"I thought you might have gone home before practice," she whispered back. "But I finally ran into Sophie, and she told me where to find you."

"Just getting some reading in before practice," Alex said. "What's going on? I'm not late, am I? I thought practice started at four?"

"That's why I'm here," Annie said, even more lit up than before. "There might not even *be* a practice."

The librarian, Mrs. Pattison, looked over at them from the desk at the front of the room, eyebrows raised in irritation.

"Let's take this outside," Alex suggested, sliding her book into the side pocket of her backpack and heaving herself up off the floor. She reached a hand down to Annie, pulling her up, and they exited the library, careful not to make unnecessary eye contact with Mrs. Pattison.

When they were out in the hall, Alex said, "What do you mean there might not be a practice? This is the first *day* of practice."

They shifted to the side, leaning against a row of lockers.

Annie took in a lot of air and then let it out. She turned to look at Alex, and Alex thought she might cry.

"Why would we practice," she said, "when there's not going to be a season?"

"What are you talking about?" Alex said. "We just had try-outs. The team is set."

Annie pulled out her phone, her fingers flying over the screen. "Look," she said, holding the phone between them.

Alex moved close to Annie, peering over her shoulder. It hadn't finished loading yet, but Alex saw at the top of the screen the link to the *Orville Patch*, their town's local paper.

Annie pointed at the big, screaming headline:

ACROSS THE BOARD SPORTS CUTBACKS
IN PUBLIC SCHOOLS

Annie scrolled through the article so Alex could read it.

The story said that because of what was called a budget "short-fall," and due to diminished contributor funding to the sports programs, the Town Council had no choice but to discontinue some sports, from the middle school through the high school.

One of the programs was seventh-grade spring soccer for girls. Their team. Their sport. Their season.

"What about the boys?" Alex said.

"*They* still get to have a team," Annie said.

I just went from reading a story I love to one I totally hate, Alex thought.

"They took our season away!" Annie said.

Alex could tell she was on the verge of tears.

"I know," Alex said, not sure what else to say in that moment.

"*No*," Annie said, "*you don't know.*"

"I'm on the team too," Alex said.

"For what?" Annie said. "Twenty minutes? If you loved soccer the way I do, you never would have quit the team."

"You know there was more to it than that," Alex said.

Annie swept a hand through her wavy brown hair and sighed. "I know," she said, more calmly now. "Sorry, I didn't mean to take this out on you. I'm just mad at the whole situation. Like, why us, you know?"

"I don't know," Alex said, because she genuinely didn't have an answer for Annie. Couldn't explain why this was happening. How she could go from being so happy one minute about making the team to now potentially not even having a team to play for.

There was nothing she could say that could make Annie feel better. Or hurt less than she clearly did right now. They stood there in silence, Annie taking deep breaths and loudly letting them out, until Alex said, "There has to be something somebody can do about this."

"There isn't," Annie said. "That's what my mom says, anyway. And she's on the board at our school."

"How did she say they decided which sports to cut and which ones to keep?" Alex asked.

"The sports that got hit the hardest were ones that attracted the fewest new members," Annie said. "They looked at how many girls tried out for spring soccer last year compared to this one."

Alex thought about that. There were only three open slots on the team this season and twelve girls at tryouts. That seemed pretty competitive to Alex.

"What about lacrosse?" Alex said.

"They had twice as many girls try out," Annie said.

"Eighth-grade girls' soccer survived the cut. But that doesn't help if you're in seventh."

"But the spring team won our league last year," Alex said.

"I *know*," said Annie.

It didn't make any logical sense. Why would the school choose to cut a team that brought in trophies and championship wins?

Annie closed her eyes, squeezing back tears, and shook her head. "Don't they understand how much these seasons mean to us?"

"What does Coach Cross think about all this?" Alex said.

Annie clicked her phone on. "We're about to find out in five minutes."

The two of them started for the gym.

"And this is all about money?" Alex said as they walked.

Annie nodded.

"They can't find the money somewhere else in the budget?"

"Mom says there isn't any extra money anywhere." She rested her hands on top of her head. "There would have been, except they realized it costs way more to build new fields for soccer and lacrosse than they thought."

Now Alex blew out some air, like steam.

"That makes no sense!" she said. "To take away soccer so they can build a new soccer *field*?"

"We have to do something," Annie said.

"Oh, we will," Alex said. She wasn't about to lose her season to a stupid budget cut.

A plan hadn't formed just yet, but Alex vowed to come up with one soon.

Just then, the boys' seventh-grade soccer team came walking down the hall, dressed in their gear, on their way into the gym.

It was unfair to think, but Alex couldn't help but feel cheated. It wasn't their fault, but the boys' team would have their season. They were going to get to do something the girls couldn't.

Alex knew that just wasn't right.

And not just when it came to soccer.

13

COACH CROSS SURPRISED THEM WHEN THEY GOT TO THE GYM, IN more ways than one, but starting with this: she didn't act as if the season had just gotten canceled. In fact, she spoke as if it were just beginning.

"Grab your jackets or parkas or hoodies or whatever," she said. "I don't think anybody would call this a beach day in Orville, but we're practicing outside today."

"Coach," Annie said. "Didn't you hear what happened? They called off seventh-grade girls' soccer. It was announced in the *Patch*."

"Why would we have practice," Lindsey said, "if we're not going to be playing any games?"

"I'm sorry," Coach said dramatically. "Did you all stop being soccer players the moment you heard the news from our illustrious Town Council?"

She was smiling—happy, even. As if nothing had changed. As if the *Orville Patch* never ran any stories on budget cuts. As if she were living in some kind of alternate universe.

Alex couldn't make heads or tails of it. They had brought her in, this local soccer legend, to coach their team. Only now there was no team.

The girls looked at each other, wondering if they should

follow Coach Cross's orders and get their jackets. Finally, Carly Jones spoke.

"You know what?" she said to her teammates. "We *are* still players. So let's go play."

As they were about to leave the gym, the double doors opened, and in walked all the girls who hadn't made the team. They already had their jackets on, and Alex could see they were also wearing shin guards over their sweatpants, and soccer cleats.

"I don't understand," Alex said to Coach Cross.

"If the best we can do is play games against each other," she said, "I figured we'd need all the players we could get."

Then she picked up the ball at her feet, bounced it off one knee, and headed for the field.

"I had a feelin' I was going to like this school," Roisin said to Alex.

They bumped fists as Alex said, "Let's do this."

She just wasn't quite sure what *this* was.

14

THEY WERE OUTSIDE NOW AND GLAD TO BE WEARING EXTRA LAYERS. The sun had disappeared behind the clouds, and the day hadn't just become grayer but also a whole lot colder.

Once on the field, though, running and passing the ball around, getting the blood flowing, Alex knew how good it felt to be back. She could see it on the faces of her teammates too. They were happy to be out here, regardless of what the news said.

After warm-ups, Coach Cross gathered everyone around her. She was holding a soccer ball under her arm. Alex noticed she always had one close by.

"Listen, I'm not going to lie," she said. "I was as shocked as all of you to hear the news today. I'd jumped at the chance to coach you guys because I had the time of my life playing here in Orville when I was a kid. Guess I just love soccer!"

"We love it too!" Carly said. "Only now we aren't going to get to play."

"But the boys are," Lindsey muttered.

"Let's be clear," Coach said. "The boys didn't do anything wrong. And I don't believe the Town Council went out of their way to single out seventh-grade girls. It's just the way things worked out. But we're going to make the most of it."

"It feels like somebody knocked us down," Annie said.

"And today we start getting back up," Coach Cross said with a boost of enthusiasm. "And by the way?" she continued. "Anybody can get knocked down. It doesn't tell the world anything about our character or our talent or our heart. You know what does? How we get back up."

Alex hung on to Coach Cross's every word.

Empowered. That's how she felt. Ready to fight.

"But now there's no league for us to play in," Ally McGee said. "How are we supposed to compete?"

"Guess we'll have to figure out a way to be our own league," Coach said.

After they had finished with their passing and shooting drills, Coach divided them up into teams, mixing and matching with the new girls and the holdovers to keep things fair.

Alex and Roisin were up front on one team with Carly in the goal. Rashida played keeper for Annie and Lindsey's side.

The field was a little slick, but they'd gotten used to it during warm-ups. And considering that only half of them had ever played together, Alex thought that the passing and teamwork was pretty strong between the teams.

It almost felt like a real game.

No one was more into it than Alex, who felt as if she'd never been away. It'd been a full year since she'd played soccer on a team, but just like riding a bike, muscle memory kicked in. It felt natural, easy. Sure, she missed open teammates early on. She missed a couple of shots too. But it was the *feeling* that had returned to her. The feeling of making a good pass. Of having a clean takeaway in the open field. Or a good tackle. A soccer tackle, not like the kind in football. In soccer that meant engaging a player on the other team and taking the ball away cleanly, even if the two of you collided.

With a minute left in the scrimmage and the score still 0–0, Alex did precisely that with Lindsey at midfield. Pretty much a perfect play, if she did say so herself. Alex slid at the exact right moment, managed to kick the ball away from Lindsey, jumped to her feet, and got control of it in one swift motion. Then passed it ahead to a streaking Roisin.

Lindsey tried to flop, even though Alex hadn't made any contact with her, throwing her arms up into the air as if Alex had just put a football tackle on her.

"Hey!" she yelled.

But from behind them Alex heard Coach Cross say, "C'mon, Lindsey. A light breeze would have had a better chance of putting you on the ground."

But by then Alex was flying after Roisin, both of them hoping to score the first goal of the game. Roisin looked to her left and saw Alex catching up with her, so she passed the ball back when she saw the open field in front of her. Then Alex was splitting two defenders, Andi Welles and Karla Morant. Roisin faded a bit, creating more separation between herself and Alex, and giving herself more room to run. Then she slowed down just a touch because even though it *was* a practice game Coach Cross had been blowing the whistle every time one of them went offsides.

Alex expertly dribbled the ball. She'd made such a good, fast move on Andi and Karla that now there was no one between Alex and Roisin and Rashida in the goal.

Let Rashida make the first move, Alex told herself.

Rashida didn't know whether Alex was passing or shooting. But Alex did.

Rashida's eyes were fixed on Alex coming toward her with the ball. Alex watched her right back, the ball on her right foot, knowing exactly where it was without having to look down.

At the last possible moment, Alex stopped and wound up with her right leg, like she was looking to drive one home.

Rashida leaned to her right, guessing from Alex's body position that she'd be going that way, putting a natural hook on the ball.

But Alex wasn't shooting. Instead, she looked down at the ball and slid it with her left foot, just a gentle nudge, over to Roisin.

Her backyard move with a twist.

All Roisin had to do was nudge the ball herself into the wide-open net to Rashida's left.

Game over at 1–0. Or one-nil, as the announcers liked to say in soccer.

Alex had no idea what would become of their team going forward, or where they were heading from here. None of them did, not even Coach Cross.

But after this one day, she knew no matter what, if they were lucky enough to have one, this would be a season to remember.

Roisin came running over, and they both jumped into the air and bumped chests.

"Now I know why you were such a good quarterback," Roisin said to her.

15

THEY PRACTICED EVERY DAY FOR THE REST OF THE WEEK AFTER school, scrimmaging with their suddenly supersized team to prepare for a season they didn't know if they'd ever have.

Every time one of them would ask Coach Cross her honest opinion about what might happen, she'd just smile and shrug and say, "Working on it," before reminding them that they were still weeks away from their first league game against Palmer.

On Friday afternoon, when practice was over, Annie asked, "But what we're doing right now could all be for nothing, right?"

"Let me ask you something, Annie," Coach said. "What we're doing every day on that field, does that feel like nothing to you? Because it doesn't *look* like nothing to me."

Annie placed her hands on her hips, catching her breath. "It's just . . . we've put in so much work," she said.

"Didn't look like work to me either," Coach said with a wink.

Gabe called the next morning to ask if Alex was up for meeting him at the middle school field to kick her soccer ball around.

"Unless you're going to be a weather weenie and say it's too cold," Gabe said.

"It *is* too cold!" she whined.

"Weenie," he said.

"You know I'm bluffing," Alex said, and told Gabe she'd meet him there.

Alex took her bike to Gabe's house, and the two of them rode over to Orville Middle. When they arrived, Alex quickly discovered the field was even slicker than it'd been at the previous day's practice. Alex even slipped a couple of times trying to plant a foot and fire a shot at Gabe in the goal, landing on her butt more times than she could count.

"Ouch?" she said to Gabe the second time it happened.

"Wait," Gabe said, "my quarterback can't take a hit? Make it make sense."

Alex got back up. Gabe came out of the goal. They got about twenty yards apart and passed the ball back and forth, trapping the ball and controlling it before kicking it back. Gabe, Alex knew, had been a tremendous soccer player himself through fifth grade before switching to baseball. Football was still his favorite sport. But now he enjoyed being a baseball pitcher almost as much.

He'd once explained to her that as much fun as soccer was, he preferred sports where you could use your hands. Now he had the best of both worlds: catching footballs and throwing baseballs.

Jabril had told her at lunch that nobody in their league threw a fastball like Gabe. He was turning thirteen in a month, which meant this summer he'd be old enough to move up from Little League to Babe Ruth, on what he called "the big field."

It was even colder today than it had been at Friday's practice, and Alex asked Gabe if he wanted to keep playing. He said he was about soccer-ed out for one Saturday morning, checking his phone and telling her it was almost time for lunch.

"Tell you what," Alex said. "We play fifteen more minutes and I'll buy us slices at Sam's."

"Can't pass up a deal like that," he said.

Alex was holding the ball now, smiling at one of her best friends in the world.

"What?" he said.

"I'm just happy to be back on a field with you," she said. "It's like we're teammates again."

"We will be soon enough."

Alex tossed him the soccer ball football-style, putting more than a little zip on it. Gabe caught it easily, of course. He wasn't kidding about using his hands. Alex figured he could probably catch a flying fish if he had the chance.

"Good to know you can still throw," Gabe said. "Now kick me a deep ball so we can see how your soccer skills measure up."

"Carlisle to Hildreth?" Alex said.

"Carlisle trying to outkick Hildreth's coverage this time!" Gabe yelled back as he took off down the field.

Before he was out of her range, she stepped into her kick and let it go with everything she had.

She thought she'd led him perfectly.

She hadn't.

The ball was a little too far in front of him. But this was Gabe. He was as competitive as she was. Even now, he refused to miss a single ball. He was *going* to catch up with it. Whatever it took.

Alex watched as he was about to extend, stretch out with his legs the way he did with his arms when the football was nearly out of reach.

Saw him take one last huge stride with his right leg.

Saw his left foot give out on the slippery field, his knee twist, and his whole leg collapse beneath him.

Alex could tell something was wrong right away.

She bolted toward him, careful not to slip on the wet ground, as Gabe cried out in pain, reaching for his left knee with both hands, clutching it to his chest.

16

GABE WAS SITTING ON THE DAMP GRASS RIGHT WHERE HE'D FALLEN. Alex squatted down next to him, keeping him still while they waited for their dads to arrive.

"I can walk," Gabe pleaded.

"I know you *can* walk," Alex said. "I'm just not going to let you."

She sat down next to him. The ground was cold, but she didn't care. All that mattered now was helping Gabe any way she could.

"This is all my fault," she said. "We should have gone right to Sam's when you wanted to. I was the one who talked you into staying out here."

Gabe had his legs stretched out in front of him. Alex noticed the grass stains on the knees of his sweats.

"You didn't make me do anything," he said. "And anyway, I'm the one who told you to kick the long ball."

She had him pull up his left pant leg, where they noticed his knee beginning to swell up. He said he might have stepped in a little divot in the field. That's when he felt his leg give out, like someone had hit him from behind with a rolling block.

Alex felt awful. Gabe was one of her closest friends and an ally on the football field. She couldn't have made it through the season without his friendship and support. Now she was worried he might have injured himself badly enough to compromise his baseball season. Possibly causing him to miss it entirely.

She was getting *way* ahead of herself. She needed to quiet her brain.

But she couldn't.

"Maybe I just pulled something," Gabe said.

Their dads were jogging toward them now, matching looks of concern on their faces.

"That's probably it," Alex said.

Please let that be all it is.

Alex and Gabe quickly told their dads what happened, and Mr. Hildreth examined his son's knee before running back to the parking lot to get his SUV. Jack and Alex stayed with Gabe while Mr. Hildreth drove his car right onto the field. Then the two men helped Gabe up and carefully lifted him into the back seat for the drive to Orville Medical Center. Alex rode in the back with Gabe, his leg extended across the seat.

She spent most of the ride staring out the window at the bare, leafless trees rolling by. Every so often, she'd glance over at Gabe, see him wincing in pain and gripping his knee whenever they hit a bump in the road.

With each bump, her guilt ratcheted up another notch.

Mr. Hildreth said that Dr. Calabrese, whose son Cal had played center for the Owls, was going to meet them in the emergency waiting room.

During football season, when Alex had taken a hard hit—a cheap shot, really—during a game, it had been Dr. Calabrese who assured her that it wasn't serious and all she really needed was ice.

Maybe it was going to be the same way with Gabe.

Alex could only hope.

She and her dad sat in the waiting area while they x-rayed Gabe's knee to ensure nothing was broken. Dr. Calabrese seemed pretty confident nothing was, from the way Gabe had explained the injury. Then they took Gabe to a different floor for an MRI, which Dr. Calabrese said would give them a better look at the anterior cruciate ligament.

The dreaded ACL.

Alex was no doctor, but she *was* a sports fan, which meant she knew that a bad ACL injury, a tear, could lead to surgery.

Her brain was racing so fast Alex imagined it giving off sparks.

The doors to the waiting area finally opened, and Gabe came out on crutches, his leg wrapped in a temporary brace to keep it stable.

Mr. Hildreth and Dr. Calabrese walked out behind him.

"What did the MRI show?" Alex said to Gabe, anxious for the news.

"Doc says the earliest, like the very earliest, we can see the scans is tomorrow," Gabe said. "He's trying to fast-track the results."

Dr. Calabrese came walking over and laid a hand on Gabe's shoulder.

"Best-case scenario, and you know I'm a best-case-scenario kinda guy," he said, "is that it's a sprain and not a tear. Just by the way he's able to move the knee, that's my guess. But we'll know tomorrow."

Alex said she'd call Gabe later, and then he and his dad

proceeded through the automatic sliding doors into the parking lot.

Alex watched them go. Then she and her dad drove home.

When they were pulling into the driveway, Jack said, "He's going to be fine. Just a question of whether it's sooner or later."

"He was doing me a favor," Alex said, getting a little choked up, "or it wouldn't have happened."

"Honey," her dad said, "you can't blame yourself."

"Who else should I blame?" she said.

He asked if she wanted some lunch, but she said she wasn't hungry.

"Y'know, not eating isn't going to help Gabe."

"Maybe later," she said. "Just need to make a call first."

"To who?" her dad asked.

"Mom."

Dr. Liza Borelli picked up on the first ring, and Alex told her what had happened. Then her mom assured her that everything Dr. Calabrese had done so far sounded exactly right, and the only thing to do now was wait for the MRI results.

"There are basically three kinds of ACL injuries," Liza explained. "Sprain. Partial tear. Complete tear. The last one requires surgery. Sometimes a partial tear does too. But just a sprain? Those heal, and sometimes fairly quickly."

"But that gives Gabe a whole extra day to be scared," Alex said.

"I haven't spent all that much time with Gabe," her mom said, "but he seems like a pretty tough kid to me."

Alex gulped, her face feeling hot all of a sudden. "But if he really did tear it, he might not just have to sit out baseball season," she said. "He could miss football too."

"Well," said her mom, "there's nothing we can do about that today."

"You could come see him," Alex said, her voice small, yet pleading.

"Dr. Calabrese is doing all the right things," her mom said. "There's nothing else I can—"

"Please, Mom," Alex said. "Just to help put Gabe at ease . . ."

So, her mom asked for Dr. Calabrese's number, which Alex pulled off the football team's contact list, and an hour and a half later she and Alex were sitting with Gabe and his parents in their living room. Gabe was on the couch, legs outstretched in front of him, crutches propped up against the nearby wall. On the coffee table was his PlayStation controller. He'd been playing *MLB The Show.*

He was wearing a pair of gym shorts and had removed his brace for now. Alex saw that his left knee was swollen and a little black and blue. Gabe said it was feeling better, but Alex wasn't so sure. She knew him well enough to know he downplayed the seriousness of injuries, even if he was in severe pain. It was just in his nature. He never wanted to be considered a burden.

Liza gently prodded around the inside and outside of the injured knee. Then Mr. and Mrs. Hildreth helped lift Gabe off the couch, each taking an arm, so he could put some weight on the leg. Liza knelt down next to him and showed them all exactly where the ligament in question was.

"That pesky anterior cruciate ligament," she said, smiling up at Gabe. "Sounds a lot simpler when you just abbreviate it."

"It's like you don't even really know you have one until you do something to it," Gabe said.

"But then it gets better," Alex's mom said. "That's what our bodies do. They heal."

Alex wasn't sure how Dr. Calabrese worked his magic, but he managed to get the MRI results back the following day, even though it was Sunday. Orville was a small town, where most everyone knew each other. The woman who ran Quest Diagnostics, Ms. Ferrell, also had a son on the football team, Bobby, who'd played linebacker alongside Jabril.

Gabe was at Alex's house when the doctor called. She'd insisted he come over so that he wouldn't have to receive the news by himself. His parents were both at work.

It was about four in the afternoon when Gabe's phone buzzed in his pocket. At first, he made no move to answer, as if avoiding the call altogether would prevent any possible bad news from existing.

"You have to answer it," Alex said.

Gabe nodded and lifted the phone to his ear.

"Hey, Doc," he said.

Alex's eyes were trained on Gabe's face as the conversation carried on, reading into every reaction. Every expression.

Gabe listened and was quiet most of the time. A few "mm-hmm"s and "uh-huh"s sprinkled throughout the call.

Alex was on pins and needles. She wished Gabe would have

put the doctor on speakerphone but knew that wouldn't have been right. This was private medical information after all, and Gabe would tell her everything anyway.

After several minutes, and a few more "okay"s and "yeah"s from Gabe, he said, "Thanks so much for everything, Doc," before hanging up the phone.

"Well?" Alex said.

Gabe slipped his phone back into his pocket and said, "Just a sprain."

No tear.

No surgery.

Alex let out a sigh of relief.

Alex's mom called about an hour later. With the permission of Gabe's parents, Dr. Calabrese had emailed her the images of Gabe's scan so she could take a closer look.

Alex put her mom on speaker so Gabe could hear. She said she noticed some slight fluid in the tendon sheath and that he ought to stay on crutches until the swelling went down. Gabe asked if he still might be ready for opening day of baseball season.

"When's that?" Alex's mom asked over the phone.

Alex grinned at Gabe. "Mom's not exactly the world's number one sports fan."

"I can hear you," she said.

Gabe told her when the Owls were supposed to play their first game—March 13. Liza said that starting now, the healing process would be up to the knee and up to Gabe. And that he might be able to lose the crutches as soon as next week.

"When can I start running again?" Gabe asked.

"Maybe light running in a few weeks," Liza said, "after Dr. Calabrese takes a few more pictures of that knee."

"It still doesn't feel great," Gabe said.

"I'm sure it doesn't," Alex's mom said. "It'll be a few more days, maybe even weeks, until it starts to feel better. But you're still allowed to feel good today."

They ended the call, and Gabe pulled up his sweatpants so they could both look at the knee. Then he bent it slightly and winced.

"I don't know about opening day," he said with a grimace.

"I do," Alex said.

"What are you, my personal trainer?"

"No," she said. "Just your personal cheerleader."

"Sophie's rubbing off on you, huh?" Gabe joked.

But Alex was serious. She might not get to have her season, but she was going to do everything in her power to make sure Gabe had his.

17

AT LUNCH ON MONDAY, SOME OF THE GIRLS ON THE SOCCER team wondered aloud if they might try another sport in the spring.

Kim Callaghan had played club lacrosse until sixth grade. So had Ellen Carr, and Lulu Werner had only given up softball the prior year.

"I'd do anything for our team," Kim said. "But if there isn't going to be a team, what's the point?"

"Right now, all we're doing is having a good time after school and getting in some exercise," Ellen said.

The team had pushed together two tables in the cafeteria and were sitting as a group for a change. The holdover players still hadn't completely embraced the new ones, but at least they could put it past them for one forty-minute lunch period.

"Listen," Alex said, "the tryouts for those other sports aren't for another week. Let's just all hang in there and see if something good happens before then."

"Like what," Carly said, twisting one of her chestnut brown curls, "somebody on the Town Council wins the lottery?"

"Ellen and Alex are right," Annie said. "We're having a good time and getting to hang with each other, so why not just hold tight for the moment?"

"Can I say something?" Lindsey said, standing at the end of her table and facing the group.

You're gonna say it anyway, whether we like it or not, Alex thought.

"I've been doing some thinking," she said. "And what I've determined is that we can't just take this lying down."

Alex looked around. Lindsey certainly knew how to command a room.

"I get that a bunch of grown-ups didn't single us out," she said. "But that doesn't mean we can let them take away our season like this."

"But they already have," Ally said.

"No," Lindsey said, a note of authority in her voice, "that's the thing. They can't officially cancel until teams in our league start playing games."

Now Annie chimed in.

"But I went to the league website last night," Annie said. "We're not even on the schedule. It's like somebody hit the delete button on the Orville Owls."

"It doesn't matter," Lindsey said. "We can un-delete ourselves if we do one thing."

She scanned her eyes across both tables, making sure she had their full attention. Then, satisfied, she said three simple words: "Raise some money."

No one said anything at first. Lindsey made it sound so simple Alex wondered why nobody had thought of it before.

Annie's hand shot into the air, like they were in a classroom and not the cafeteria.

"We could do one of those GoFundMe things!" she said, but they all politely shot that one down.

"I always thought about that as something you used for people who were sick, or in need," Rashida said.

"'Shida's right," Annie said. "We want a season, but we don't *need* a season."

"Or we could just ask our parents to chip in," Lindsey said.

Alex wasn't so sure about that idea. Lindsey came from an affluent family. It'd be no big deal to ask her mom and dad for cash. But others weren't in a position to do that.

However, Alex had to admit Lindsey was on the right track and had clearly done her research.

"I went online to get a sense of how much money it would cost to fund a seventh-grade soccer team," she said. Then she pulled out a piece of paper and started listing off the things the money would cover: insurance, referees, buses to road games, a doctor and an EMT van at all of their home games, even Coach Cross's salary if she'd accept one. But the more Lindsey read, the more Alex's heart started to sink right under the table. There was more to it than she had ever realized. She knew Orville was a wonderful town in which to grow up. But it wasn't a rich town, not by a long shot.

Alex felt as if she were suddenly getting a tutorial, from Lindsey of all people, about how much sports actually cost, when they'd all grown up taking sports for granted.

"I've probably forgotten some things," Lindsey said when she finished. "But still: if each of us could come up with a certain amount, I think we could do this."

The girls all whispered to each other, their spirits visibly lifting. This was all sounding possible now, within reach.

Until a loud voice carried over all the others.

"No!"

Alex was shocked to discover it was her own.

18

THE OTHER GIRLS ON THE TEAM SUDDENLY GOT QUIET, AND ABOUT twenty pairs of eyes turned to stare at her.

Lindsey, who was hardly her best friend to begin with, scowled at Alex.

Alex had never considered herself a loud person by any means. But she had been undeniably loud just then.

Lindsey had her hands on her hips.

"I'm sorry, Alex," she said. "Did you want to share some of your insights with the rest of us?"

Alex tried not to let her embarrassment show.

"I didn't mean to interrupt . . ." she began.

"Except that's exactly what you did," Lindsey said. "Apparently you think my idea is dumber than rocks."

Alex reluctantly stood up. "No," she said, "that's not it, Lindsey. I think trying to come up with the money is a great idea."

"Didn't sound that way to me," Lindsey said. "So why don't you explain to us what the problem is?"

Alex breathed in. "There's no problem except . . ." she said. "I think we should try to raise the money ourselves, you know? Instead of, um, asking people for donations."

"And I suppose you have a brilliant idea for how to do that?" Lindsey said.

Alex couldn't help herself. She laughed.

"I have no clue," she said.

"So basically, you don't like my plan, but you don't have one of your own? How does *that* work?"

Alex took another deep breath.

"Lindsey," she said quietly, not wanting to sound as if they were having an argument, "we're on the same team here. We want the same thing."

"Oh, you mean now that you want to be on the team again?" Lindsey said. "Good timing, by the way."

"I want us to have a team because all of us here have a chance to be great," Alex said. "But if we're going to do this, we need to do it right. Which means we need to own it."

"Let's go!" Roisin cheered.

Lindsey pinned her eyes on Roisin, but Annie cut off whatever she was about to say.

"Let Alex finish," she said.

Right then, Alex caught Sophie walking over from the other side of the cafeteria. She gave Alex a wink. It was enough to encourage Alex to continue.

"Just because we don't have the Town Council behind us doesn't mean we can't figure out a way to get the *town* behind us," Alex said. "This is just my opinion, but I don't believe we should go looking around for handouts, not even from our parents. We've got to come up with an idea for how to raise the money ourselves."

"But we're already running out of time," Lindsey said. "I still think my way is better."

"We don't have to decide this today," Alex said. "Let's everybody try to come up with some ideas over the rest of the week. No such thing as a bad idea. And if nothing works out, I'll shut up and we can do it Lindsey's way."

Lindsey still didn't look happy. She took a long time before responding, as if she'd suddenly appointed herself acting captain of the team.

But finally, to Alex's surprise, she agreed.

The bell rang, signaling the end of lunch, and Alex joined up with Sophie and Roisin before exiting the cafeteria.

Sophie looped an arm through Alex's elbow and said, "Well, here comes another Hail Mary pass from the one and only Alex Carlisle."

19

ALEX WAS HAVING PIZZA WITH SOPHIE, GABE, AND JABRIL AT SAM'S that Saturday afternoon.

Dr. Calabrese had swung by Gabe's house in the morning to drop off a brace for his knee. He was still limping slightly but seemed relieved to no longer need crutches. Alex had even suggested a light game of catch later, but Gabe said he was nowhere near being ready for that.

"How's the knee feel?" Sophie said to Gabe.

"I'll handle that one," Jabril said. "I asked him the same thing when my dad drove us over here." He grinned. "It didn't go well."

"Um," Gabe said. "It didn't *not* go well."

"Unless you were the one asking the question," Jabril muttered under his breath.

"All I said was that if one more person asked me how I felt, my head was going to explode."

"But Sophie just did," Alex said, "and your head looks fine to me."

Their pizzas arrived at the table. One medium cheese for Alex and Jabril. A large pepperoni for Gabe and Sophie, who both had appetites the size of the entire pizzeria.

"So," Alex said now to Gabe, "how's the knee?"

He laughed along with the rest of them, shaking his head.

As they ate, they discussed Lindsey's idea about the girls raising money. At one point Jabril said to Alex, "Can I ask you something?"

"Shoot."

"What's the difference who gives you the money?" he said. "Whether they're your parents, or donations, or whatever. It's all gravy as long as it comes from somewhere, right?"

Alex paused long enough to fork a piece of pepperoni from Gabe's plate.

"I know this might not make sense," Alex said, "but if we get the money from our parents or relatives, it'll almost be like they're buying us a team instead of us earning it ourselves."

"She's right," Sophie said, biting into her second slice of pizza.

Jabril nodded, understanding Alex's point of view now. "So all you have to do is come up with a better plan than Lindsey's?"

He said it as though it were as easy as pie.

"It's not like I'm trying to compete against Lindsey," Alex clarified. "More that I think we can take her idea and make it even better."

They ate in silence, each thinking of ways the soccer team might raise the money.

"I've got it!" Sophie said, once she'd cleared her plate. "A bake sale!"

They all stared at her, the way most of the people at Sam's suddenly were.

"That's it?" Jabril said. "That's your idea? You're gonna save the season with cookies?"

"Don't be silly," Sophie said. "Brownies too." She playfully nudged Jabril in the side. "No, for real—the cheerleaders sometimes hold school-wide bake sales to raise money for championship entrance fees. We usually make a lot of dough . . . pun intended."

"Sophie," Alex said, "you know I love you. But we'd need to host like fifty bake sales to even come close to raising enough money."

"That's a lot of cookies . . ." Gabe said.

"I guess you're right," Sophie said, "but keep it in your back pocket."

They kicked around some other ideas, but none of them amounted to much. Jabril eventually suggested a raffle, which didn't sound like a terrible idea. But when Alex asked what they could raffle off—

"How about a car?" he said.

Now they all glared at him.

"Dude," Gabe said. "Where do you plan on getting a free car?"

Jabril shrugged. "Perry Moses's dad sells cars."

Perry was one of their football teammates. His dad worked at the Ford dealership in Orville.

"They're not just gonna donate a car," Gabe said.

"Hey," Jabril said, "crazier things have happened."

When they had all chipped in to pay for the pizza, Sophie suggested they go for ice cream. Alex asked if she thought ice cream might help them come up with an idea.

"Well," Sophie said, "it certainly couldn't hurt."

It was when they were outside, on their way to Bostwick's, that they saw Chase Gwinn heading in their direction with Johnny Gallotta, one of his teammates on the boys' seventh-grade soccer team.

Chase wasn't just the best boys' player their age in Orville, he was one of the best in this part of Pennsylvania. He played center middie. Johnny played on his right.

Alex hadn't spent much time around Chase, but she loved watching him play when she checked out the boys' games. But Sophie was always talking about how cocky he was. Alex didn't know him well enough to know if he was or wasn't. She'd always had a hard time knowing where confidence stopped and cockiness began.

She'd asked Gabe one time if he liked Chase, and he'd said, "Almost as much as he likes himself."

In addition to playing for Orville Middle in the fall, Chase also played in a travel league. Sophie, who seemed to know everything that was happening with everybody at their school, said that playing on both teams meant he was practicing or competing almost every single day.

Alex hadn't seen many of his games last fall because she was so busy with football. But when she had watched him play, she'd noticed that he was usually the fastest player on the field and always seemed to have the ball on a string. To top it off, he had the innate ability to know where everybody was on the field at once. Even the players behind him.

"Hey, you guys," Chase said to them.

There was a lot of fist-bumping all around as they greeted each other.

"Sorry to hear about the soccer deal," he said to Alex. "That totally stinks."

"We've been trying to figure out a way to raise money to fund the season ourselves," Alex said.

Chase shrugged. "Well," he said, "you're a football star now. You'll be fine, right?"

He makes it seem like it's no big deal.

"It's not just about me," she said. "It's about every player on the team."

"But spring soccer isn't as important as fall soccer, right?" he said. "That's what everybody considers the real season."

"Is that how you feel about your team?" Sophie asked.

"Soccer's never out of season for me," he said, a little smugly.

Alex knew that Sophie couldn't stop herself from being Sophie.

"Well," she said to Chase, "think about how you'd feel if your season were canceled."

"Luckily we don't have to," Johnny said. "Our season's still happening."

Alex had heard of people having ESP and could swear she felt Sophie's anger coursing through her own body.

Then Chase turned to Alex and said, "I hear you're pretty good. You know, it's not too late for you to try out for our team."

It was an underhanded compliment, and frankly, Alex didn't care. She didn't have time for playing games, unless they were soccer games.

"Happy where I am, thanks," Alex replied, putting some snap into her voice.

She hadn't expected their run-in with Chase and Johnny to turn so awkward so quickly. But it had. Probably because they failed to express any sympathy for the girls losing their season. So long as they had theirs, nothing else mattered.

"Alex's team would've probably turned out even better than yours by the end of the season," Jabril remarked.

Chase's lips turned upward into a nasty grin. "Wait," he said. "You're serious?"

"I've watched them practice a few times," Jabril said. "They look good enough to win a championship to me."

"You seem to know a lot about soccer for a football player," Chase said.

Jabril winked at Chase. "I know a lot of things about a lot of things."

"Well," Chase said, "if we need a practice scrimmage before the start of our *actual* season, I'll tell our coach to call up Coach Cross."

Is that his way of being nice? Alex wondered.

"We've got enough players to scrimmage every day," Alex said. "But thanks for the idea."

"If you're not going to have a season, why bother?" Johnny said.

"Love of the game?" Alex said, and then brushed them off, saying they needed to hurry if they were going to make it to Bostwick's before their parents came to pick them up.

When they were halfway up the block, Jabril said, "What the heck was *that* all about?"

"I know," Sophie said.

ESP, Alex thought.

20

BOSTWICK'S WAS ALL THE WAY ON THE OTHER SIDE OF DOWNTOWN, on Elm Street, a walk of about six blocks. Alex asked Gabe if it was too long for him, and he said he was so glad to be off crutches, he was willing to walk all the way home. His only request was that they take it slow, and Jabril, Sophie, and Alex were happy to oblige.

"Chase's sister is on the squad with me," Sophie said. "She's still only in sixth grade, but she's really good."

Gabe grinned. "Good as you?"

"I'll ignore that," Sophie said.

"Withdraw the question," Gabe said, with his hands up in defense.

"*Anyway*," Sophie continued, "she told me one time that Chase was peeved about Alex sucking up all the attention by playing football. He was having a banner season in soccer, but all anybody in town wanted to talk about was Alex playing quarterback."

"I actually heard the same thing," Jabril said, "but it sounded so silly I didn't think it was worth talking about."

"Well," Sophie said, rolling her eyes, "apparently it was to Chase, God's gift to soccer."

Alex couldn't believe what she was hearing.

"You're telling me that Chase was jealous? Of *me*?"

"Don't act so surprised," Jabril said with a laugh.

"But I never did anything to him," Alex said, still confused. "I barely talk to him."

"*We* know that," Sophie said. "I'm just telling you he thinks *you* took the spotlight away from him."

The whole thing sent Alex's head whirling.

They had finally arrived at Bostwick's. Gabe hadn't complained about his knee during the walk, but he seemed relieved to finally sit down in a booth across from the counter.

"So Chase is gloating that our season is canceled because he's got some kind of personal grudge against me?" Alex said. "That makes no sense."

"I'm not *totally* sure, but it seems likely," Sophie said. "Just given the facts."

"It's not like I'm in some kind of competition with him," Alex said.

"He decided you were last fall," Sophie said, "whether you were aware of it or not. He thought he should be the star of everything, and then you were."

Jabril had gone up to the counter to pick up their orders. Sophie called over and told him not to forget extra sprinkles for hers.

"You know what I think," Gabe said. "Maybe you guys should take him up on his offer to scrimmage. I'd pay to see you on the same field, taking them down in person."

Jabril walked slowly back to their table, carrying a tray with their orders. It was then that they dropped the Chase conversation and concentrated on their ice cream instead.

But when Alex was home an hour later, she did something she'd never done in her life.

She called Lindsey Stiles.

Though that wasn't the only surprise of the afternoon.

The second was that when Alex asked if she could come over, Lindsey didn't say no.

"I'll explain when I get there," Alex said, and hung up.

21

LINDSEY LIVED CLOSE ENOUGH THAT ALEX COULD RIDE HER BIKE TO her house. Her parents used to host get-togethers for the soccer team last year, so Alex had been there several times and knew the way.

Jack told her not to stay too long, reminding Alex that her mom was coming over for dinner.

"You're actually going to see Lindsey?" he said. "Your nemesis?"

"My *teammate*," Alex said, throwing on her coat.

He raised an eyebrow. "You've got that look," he said.

"What look?" Alex said, trying to sound innocent.

"The one you get when you're on a mission."

When she got to the Stileses' house, she rang the bell and Mrs. Stiles answered the door.

"Alex!" she said. "So nice to see you again. I never got the chance to tell you in person how proud I was of what you did on that football team last season."

"Thanks, Mrs. Stiles," Alex said, pleasantly surprised that while both her daughter and nephew were less pleased about Alex's showing on the football team, at least Mrs. Stiles was supportive.

Alex looked past Mrs. Stiles then and saw Lindsey on her way down the steps from the second floor. She wasn't smiling, but she wasn't scowling either. It was a neutral expression. Probably to appease her mom until she was out of the room.

Then it occurred to Alex: *I'm at Lindsey Stiles's house. Lindsey. Stiles's. House.*

Suddenly, a feeling of panic overwhelmed her, but it was too late to back out now.

Talk about Hail Mary passes.

"Hey, Alex," Lindsey said.

"Hey," Alex replied.

They just stood there, Lindsey on the stairwell, Alex at the front door, looking at each other until Mrs. Stiles made some excuse to leave and scurried into the kitchen.

Could this be any more awkward? Alex thought.

But she had come this far.

"Come in," Lindsey said. "I'll grab my jacket and we can sit on the back patio. There's still enough sun left."

Lindsey led Alex through the ground floor of the house, and together, they walked into the expansive backyard, which Alex noticed was about three times the size of her own.

But what she also noticed was that Lindsey had the same soccer goal as Alex set up in the grass, with a few balls scattered about.

Same sport. Same team. Same grade at school.

We've got so much in common, Alex thought. *So how did we end up this far apart?*

They sat down on wicker chairs. The furniture looked like what Alex thought someone might find in one of those swanky catalogs.

"So what's up?" Lindsey said. "It must be important for you to show up here."

Alex wasted no time. "I think I might have come up with something."

Then she told Lindsey about running into Chase and what he'd said.

"If it's not about Chase and how many goals he's scoring," Lindsey said, "he tends to lose interest in the conversation."

Some common ground, Alex thought.

"Not a fan, then?" Alex asked.

"Just of his skills," Lindsey said. "Not gonna lie. I wish I could play like that."

Alex nodded.

"Did you come over here to talk about Chase?" she said, as if Alex were already wasting her time.

Alex smiled. "It's related to Chase."

"I don't understand," Lindsey said.

"It's about an idea he had. About us scrimmaging against the boys' team," Alex said. "They can't play eleven-on-eleven because they don't have as many players as we do."

Lindsey made a snorting noise. "Yeah," she said, "they don't have every guy in the seventh grade on their team."

Alex knew enough to let that go. She wasn't here to debate Lindsey. She was trying to get them on the same side, and not just on the field.

"It was what Gabe said to me after Chase walked away. Something like, *I'd like to see you on the field with that guy*," Alex said.

"Oh my god!" Lindsey said. "Now you want to play on another boys' team! *That's* what you came over here to tell me?"

Alex put her hands up in surrender.

"No!" she said. She couldn't even stop a laugh from coming out of her. "That is absolutely *not* why I'm here."

"So why are you?"

"What if there was a way for our team to play theirs for real? Get to do some real playing this season?" Alex said.

"They'd crush us," Lindsey said, as if it were a no-brainer. "They went undefeated last fall, if you remember. What would even be the point of a game like that?"

"I'm not sure they would," Alex said. "Crush us, I mean. We've got so much talent on our team—"

"You mean now that you're back with us?" Lindsey said.

That one Alex couldn't let go.

"Lindsey," she said, "come *on*. This isn't about the two of us. This is about all of us. And if we can't find a way to work together, starting with you and me, then we're not going to get to play this spring. At least not the way we want."

Lindsey stood up then and faced the goal in her yard, arms crossed in front of her, as if deciding what she wanted to say next. In that moment, Alex started to think she had wasted her time. And wondered if anything would ever really change between them.

But here was the real wonder:

When Lindsey turned around, she was grinning ear to ear.

"Genius," she said.

"Ex*cuse* me?"

"My mom always tells me that the thing about a really good idea," Lindsey said, "is that once one gets inside your head, it's impossible to get it out."

Alex waited.

"You're saying it's genius to get on the field with those guys?" Alex asked her. "I thought it was just something we could kick around."

"Kick around, Alex?" Lindsey said. "Really?"

"Just slipped out," she said. "Okay, so can you explain how, exactly, this is a genius plan? I mean, I thought it was decent at best—"

"We're going to challenge them to a game," Lindsey said. "And we're going to get the school and the town behind it. And we're going to sell tickets and get sponsors."

Now Alex smiled, following Lindsey's train of thought. "And raise enough money to have a season . . ."

Lindsey nodded, and for the first time in a long time put out her fist for Alex to bump.

"You think they'll say yes?" Alex said.

Lindsey flashed Alex a conspiratorial look.

"How can they say no?"

Before Alex left, they decided not to tell any of their teammates, or Coach Cross, until practice on Monday.

"We should actually tell Coach before we tell anybody else," Alex said. "Just in case she thinks it's a terrible idea."

"Which it's not," Lindsey said.

"Still . . . we don't want the rest of our grade to find out before it's a done deal," Alex said. "Or the school, for that matter.

We're gonna need a lot of people on board to actually make this happen."

Lindsey nodded.

"But it can't happen if Coach Cross isn't on board," Lindsey said. "Got it."

"Soooo, between us for now?"

"What," Lindsey said, "worried about my big mouth?"

Alex laughed. So maybe Lindsey did have a sense of humor about herself after all. At least for now, they'd proven they could be cordial to each other. Even go as far as work together toward a common goal. It was more than Alex could've hoped for when she first entered Lindsey's house that afternoon.

As they got up so Lindsey could walk her out, Alex nodded toward the soccer net in the backyard.

"Hey," Alex said, "I've got that same one at home."

"You want to kick a ball around before you go?" Lindsey asked.

The fact that Lindsey had asked was proof enough for Alex that they were finally turning a corner in their relationship. It could almost be considered a peace offering.

Without thinking too hard about it, Alex took Lindsey up on her offer and ran into the goal, taking a keeper stance.

Lindsey started dribbling the ball and taking shots.

It didn't feel natural, exactly, but it was a step in the right direction.

22

ALEX AND LINDSEY ARRANGED TO MEET WITH COACH CROSS fifteen minutes before practice in the gym on Monday.

The temperature outside was in the fifties and the sun had been high in the sky all day, so Coach had emailed the team before school, letting them know they'd be having their scrimmage outdoors that afternoon.

She also hinted that she might have a surprise for them.

So do we, Alex thought.

When they met with Coach Cross in her office, Alex let Lindsey do most of the talking. She didn't care who got credit for the idea and mostly just thought that if Lindsey felt in control, she'd be more engaged and more involved as they proceeded with their plan. Lindsey preferred taking the lead, and since—for the first time—she and Alex were seeing eye to eye, it hardly mattered which of them assumed that role.

"We think we may have come up with a way to raise money to have a season," Lindsey said.

"Who's 'we'?" Coach said.

"Alex and me for now," Lindsey said. "But we think the other girls on the team will go along once we tell them our idea. Unless you think for any reason we shouldn't go through with it."

"I'm listening," Coach said.

"It's only a rough idea for now," Alex prefaced. "But we're pretty sure the girls will help us flesh it out."

Then Lindsey took the floor, explaining the basic concept.

Coach listened, remaining expressionless until Lindsey finished.

"Our team against their team," she said, capping off her speech.

"Maybe the Saturday before our season's supposed to start," Alex added.

She felt as if she and Lindsey had just co-written an essay and were waiting for Coach Cross to grade it.

"I don't like it," she said.

Alex felt her heart sink into her stomach. She eyed Lindsey, who also looked like she'd just swallowed a soccer ball.

Then Coach Cross's mouth curved upward into a wide grin, like the lights in the gym had suddenly turned up. "I love it."

"Really?" Lindsey said, blowing out the breath she'd clearly been holding for the last few seconds.

"Love, love, *love* it," Coach repeated.

Alex and Lindsey high-fived each other.

Another first.

"And I think the other girls are going to love it too," Coach said. "But they're not the only ones we'll have to convince. First, we've got to get permission from the school and the Town Council. And that might not even be the hardest part."

"What's the hardest part?" Alex said, almost afraid to ask.

"Getting Coach Selmani and the boys to buy in," she said.

Lindsey said to Coach Cross the same thing she'd told Alex only days before.

"But how can they say no? Wouldn't it make them look like they're afraid to play us?"

"It would," Coach said. "But I'm not a mind reader with seventh-grade boys." She grinned. "Or, I should say, *especially* with seventh-grade boys."

"What about the Town Council?" Lindsey said.

"I honestly believe they'd have a hard time explaining to good old Orville, Pennsylvania, why they shouldn't support an idea that would do this much good for two dozen seventh-grade girls. Not to mention that getting the community to rally around a worthy cause is good for morale."

It was settled then. Coach Cross would help get the idea in front of the proper committees, while Alex and Lindsey were responsible for telling their teammates.

But now was not the time.

Because right now was reserved for soccer.

Alex and Lindsey decided to tell the rest of the team in the locker room after practice. That way, they could focus 100 percent of their energy on soccer, then commit 100 percent of their brains to formulating a plan.

As they walked out of the gym, Alex skipped ahead to catch up with Coach Cross.

"One last question," she said. "Do you think if we play them, we have a chance to win?"

"We're going to win just by playing the game," Coach said.

"Sometimes sports don't have to be about anything more than that."

"But it sure would be fun to find out if we *can* beat them," Alex said.

"Oh, heck yeah," Coach said.

23

ONCE IN THE LOCKER ROOM, ALEX AND LINDSEY SAT EVERYONE down on the benches to tell them about their grand plan.

The words were barely out of Lindsey's mouth when the group erupted in hoots and hollers, their voices echoing loudly against the cinder-block walls. In fact, there was so much cheering, it sounded as if they'd just won a championship.

But then Coach stepped in, not to spoil their excitement but to remind everyone this wasn't set in stone. Before they got too far ahead of themselves, and before anybody else at Orville Middle found out what they were planning, she would first have to approach the head of school tomorrow. If she got the green light, her next move would be to call Mrs. McMahon, the president of the Town Council and an old high school soccer teammate of hers.

"So this has to be our secret until I have those two conversations," she said. "Understood?"

She was firm in her delivery but smiled to show she wasn't trying to be too tough on them.

"That won't be a challenge for this group, right?" she added.

Everyone nodded.

"The last thing I'd want to do is sabotage our chances of having a season," Annie spoke up.

"Exactly," Carly said. "It's in our best interest to keep our mouths zipped."

Roisin raised a hand then.

"Coach," she said, "was this the surprise you mentioned in your email this morning?"

Coach shook her head.

"Nope," she said. "My surprise is a little different."

The girls sat in silence, waiting for Coach Cross to reveal her big secret.

"How would you feel if I told you that tomorrow afternoon, we are going to scrimmage the Palmer Lions right here on our home turf?"

Cheering immediately filled the room. A few of the girls even got up to dance around, unable to contain their excitement.

For a Monday, it was turning out to be a pretty good day, Alex thought.

Maybe the first of many.

Sometimes a little luck went a long way.

24

A<small>LEX SAT WITH</small> S<small>OPHIE,</small> R<small>OISIN, AND</small> R<small>ASHIDA AT LUNCH THE NEXT</small>
day. The girls had become close ever since soccer tryouts and
could now consider themselves actual friends instead of just
"soccer buddies." And because Sophie was Alex's friend, and got
along with everybody, they all seemed to fit perfectly.

"I still don't get how the spelling of your name translates to
'Ro-sheen,'" Rashida said.

"Ah, it's just an Irish thing, isn't it?" Roisin said. "I've got a
cousin named Siobhan."

"'Shiv-on'—that's a beautiful name," Alex said. "How do you
spell that one?"

Roisin laughed. "I'd have you guess, but it's an Irish spelling.
S-I-O-B-H-A-N."

"And you call soccer 'football,'" Sophie said.

"To be fair," Alex cut in, "so does the rest of the world."

"Well, we do use our feet, yeah?" Roisin said. "Makes a whole
lot more sense to me."

"You got us there," Sophie said. "Maybe we should start calling it football."

"Well," Alex said, "whatever we call it, we've got a big game
today."

The girls on the team were keeping their promise, at least so far. No one had breathed a word about the girls vs. boys game. There had been nothing on social media, mainly because Lindsey had been watching everybody like a hawk. And by the end of the day, Coach would have talked to the school and then, hopefully, the Town Council.

But for now they were focused on the chance to play against a real opponent. One that felt big. Significant. A good omen for a season that might not be so far out of reach.

Alex refused to call it a scrimmage. The *game* was scheduled for right after school, as soon as the Palmer bus arrived in Orville. Alex and her teammates were already on the field warming up when they saw the bus pull into the parking lot behind the gym. Even that felt exciting.

As the players came down the steps, Alex saw that they were already in their orange jerseys, wearing them over long-sleeved shirts and sweaters and vests, as the day had grown colder. Some even had hoodies on. Most wore sweatpants.

Since the Orville Owls didn't have uniforms, they were wearing blue pinnies over their own sweaters and vests and hoodies.

"We're going to look so unofficial in pinnies," Lindsey said.

"I'll admit, it's not the best look," Annie said, but then she might have been the most fashion-conscious girl in their grade.

"Only until we score our first goal," Alex said. "Then we're going to look cooler than Megan Rapinoe."

"Palmer beat us in the championship game," Lindsey said to

Alex, with some snap in her voice. "I know you were off doing something else at the time . . ."

Things were better between them, but hardly great. Alex knew they were never going to be perfect, and things could turn sour at a moment's notice. Like they were right now.

"I remember," Alex said. Then she added, "But that was last year."

The championship game had come down to penalty kicks. It had been tied at the end of regulation and then into overtime. After that, the refs agreed to determine the game with PKs. Palmer selected their best player, Adella Martinez, who took the last shot and beat out Carly in the net.

Now here they were. As hopeful as Alex was to get their season back, she also knew this game might be the closest Orville got to a rematch this year.

Both teams took a ten-minute warm-up. Then the coaches called their players over to the sidelines.

"We play like champions today," Coach Cross said, keeping her voice low. "And for those of you who were on the team last season, I want you to clear your heads of that championship game. Today's a new day. We're a new team."

Alex caught Annie and Lindsey glancing at each other.

"If we do end up having a season," Coach Cross went on, "we'll be playing them in our first game. So win, lose, or tie today, let's give them something to think about. Like always, we play the game right. Next pass. Next shot. Next stop."

They didn't get the first score. Adella did, in the first minute, on a breakaway. Then Annie lost the ball to Adella at midfield a few minutes later. Adella made a sweet pass up the field to one of her other strikers, and the ball snuck in under the crossbar, just over Carly's outstretched hand.

It was 2–0 and the Owls had yet to break a sweat.

And it had nothing to do with the cold weather.

25

ALEX HADN'T STARTED THE GAME. NOT THAT SHE EXPECTED TO.

Coach had pulled the new girls aside and told them she was starting all of last year's players out of respect.

"You don't have to explain anything to me, Coach," Alex said. "The team comes first."

The starters kept the score to 2–0 after that. But twenty minutes into the game, with ten left in the half, Coach started mixing in new players, two or three at a time. The first two were Alex and Roisin, replacing Annie and Lindsey. As she ran out onto the field, Alex worried how Annie might react, even if it was only a glorified scrimmage to most. Alex never had anything against Annie, not even when she'd aligned herself with Lindsey against Alex in the fall. Though back then, it seemed everyone in the school was against her.

However, as Annie came running past Alex now, she slapped her a low five and said, "See if you can get us back into this."

"Gonna try," Alex said.

These weren't drills in the gym now. This wasn't the Owls playing against each other in a game that would never show up in any standings. They were playing against a legit league team. One they'd face in a real season, if they managed to have one. The thought got Alex thinking briefly about the prospect of playing against the guys. They needed that game more than anything.

As soon as the whistle blew, Alex snapped her attention back to the field.

All at once, she was a soccer player again. Playing against the Palmer Lions. And it felt good.

No, she thought, *check that*.

It felt *awesome*, even lined up against somebody as talented as Adella Martinez.

Coach said it didn't take long to identify the player on the other team you had the most to worry about. She was right about that.

"I thought you were a football player," Adella said to Alex after another whistle.

She didn't say it meanly. In fact, she almost sounded impressed.

"Not today," Alex said, giving her hamstring a quick stretch before Ms. Rossovich, the Palmer head coach, placed the ball on the ground between them.

Adella was fast. Really fast. So was Alex. But despite all the practices they'd had up till now, Alex knew right away that she hadn't reached peak game shape. She wasn't *Adella* fast. At least not yet.

Adella kept beating her to the ball, taking ownership of the field the way a good center middie was supposed to. They were supposed to score too. And set up scoring with their passing. In their offensive end, the game was meant to flow through them. But Coach said the place where a center middie should really show off her stuff was in the middle of the field. More like the forty-yard field *within* a field, the place where they could turn defense into offense on a dime.

Adella was doing that now, and a lot better than Alex was. In fact, at full steam, the best Alex could do was try to keep up with Adella. Outrunning her was out of the question.

Five minutes after Alex came into the game, Adella made a great defensive play against her, a clean, sliding takeaway. Before Alex knew what was happening, Adella was up on her feet again, flying toward Carly and scoring her second goal of the game, left-footed this time.

Now it was 3–0.

So much for getting the Owls back into it.

Alex felt like she was back at QB and had just thrown a bad interception that resulted in a touchdown for the other team.

"I'm not good enough to play with that girl," Alex said to Roisin in frustration, when they were jogging back to midfield.

"Oh, don't be an eejit," Roisin said, smiling and looking awfully upbeat considering the score.

Alex couldn't help but smile back. "Does that mean what I think it means?"

"Just like it sounds," Roisin confirmed. "Now let's crack on, shall we?"

"Need a little help with that one," Alex said.

"It means it's time for us to get on with it, yeah?"

A minute later, Alex was able to dig up some extra energy from the reserves and push herself to the max. Now she was the one turning defense into offense, catching Adella from behind and sliding to kick the ball away while avoiding direct contact. Then she got up, regained control of the ball, wheeled, and headed for Palmer's goal.

Roisin was to her right, and suddenly there was nothing but green grass stretched in front of them. What was it the football announcers said? Running in space. Alex and Roisin were running in space now.

Two defenders were positioned between them and the keeper. Palmer had been playing a 4-4-2 alignment the whole game, same as the Owls. The defender closest to Alex, a girl with a long dark braid trailing down her back, came up to try to stop her. The other defender fanned out to her left, readying herself should Alex pass to Roisin.

And it was in this moment that something happened. Something that reminded Alex why she loved sports.

She made a move she didn't know she could.

She put on the brakes and spun around so her back was to the defender and the Palmer goal.

Then she faked a pass to Roisin with her right foot before spinning to her left.

It made the girl with the braid slip and fall in an effort to keep up.

Roisin was still there on her right, except now the defender covering her was scrambling to get between Alex and the goal, doing her best to stop her from shooting on their keeper.

Alex could have taken the shot.

But Roisin had a better one, with no one there to block her.

Alex passed her the ball, and Roisin cut loose with the hardest shot she'd made since they'd started playing together that day at tryouts, catching it so cleanly Alex was surprised it didn't put a hole in the netting.

It was their only goal so far.

But to them, it may as well have been the winning score.

Roisin came running over. She jumped into Alex's arms, and Alex lifted her off the ground while Roisin pumped a fist in the air.

"You about *slagged* me with that spin move," Roisin said when Alex set her down.

"Gonna assume that's a good thing," Alex said.

"Doncha know it."

They were back in the game.

Maria Ochoa, one of the girls who'd originally been cut, turned out to be a terrific defender. She moved up right before halftime, took a pass from Roisin, and blasted a shot of her own past the Palmer goalkeeper from thirty yards away.

Just like that, 3–2, Palmer.

Now the game had *really* gotten real.

26

ALEX THOUGHT COACH MIGHT STICK WITH THE GROUP THAT HAD gotten the Owls back on track for the second half, but she decided to go back to her starters, which meant the starters from last fall.

Before the game, when Alex, Lindsey, and Annie had been standing with Coach, Lindsey asked if she might think about cutting down their roster if they did have a season.

"Nope," Coach Cross said. "Our team is our team."

"You don't think we have too many players?" Lindsey asked, trying to sound innocent.

But Alex picked up on Lindsey's apprehension. She thought having more girls on the team could threaten her play time.

"You can never have too many players," Coach replied.

Early in the second half, Adella scored again, taking the ball from Lindsey and making a quick push pass to the striker on her left. When she got the ball back, she took off, straight down the middle of the field. Made about three terrific moves, broke in on Carly, and scored easily. Right foot to Carly's left, low to the ground, a bullet.

It was 4–2, with the Lions tugging back the momentum they'd temporarily lost.

The score stayed that way until the coaches blew their whistles to signal ten minutes left. This time Coach Cross didn't bring in eleven new players. Just switched around some of the backs and made up a frontline of Alex, Annie, and Roisin.

"Who plays in the middle?" Annie asked.

"You do," said Coach.

To Annie's credit she said, "Alex played better than I did there in the first half."

"So now I've got two great center middies," Coach said. "Am I a lucky duck or what?"

The evening had gotten colder and overcast. It was one of those days, Alex thought, when winter said to spring: *Not so fast.* But Alex wasn't cold. As soon as she was back out there, heat coursed through her body from all the adrenaline. It was a good game and even better competition. Now it was all about digging deep and figuring out a way to win the game. She hadn't felt this competitive streak since football. It wasn't until now that she realized how much she'd missed it.

It took a couple of minutes to find their rhythm, but once she and Annie started to anticipate each other's movements, they were unstoppable. It was like ESP again. They didn't have to worry about Roisin, who seemed to have the best feel for soccer out of all of them. She was wherever they needed her to be.

They were clicking, even if they hadn't produced a goal.

There was a scramble for the ball almost exactly at midfield. Annie came up with it, and Roisin took off down the left side. Annie found her with an almost perfect long pass. Then Roisin collected the ball, staying onside, and drew the goalkeeper toward her, somehow finding an angle into the upper corner.

Palmer 4, Orville 3.

Plenty of time left against the team that had won the championship of the league only a few months prior. The sides looked as even as they could, even if the Owls were still down a goal.

Rashida replaced Carly in the goal with five minutes left in the game, making a great save on Adella to keep the score 4–3. Alex ran past Coach Cross.

"How much time left?" she asked.

"Four minutes" was Coach's reply.

There was still enough daylight, Alex thought. Still too much left between them and Palmer. And suddenly it was the Owls who were forcing the action now, dominating control of the ball. It seemed as if the game was mostly being played in front of the Palmer goal.

Alex was sure she had one ball behind her, but their keeper made an unbelievable diving save.

Two minutes left.

Still 4–3.

Sixty seconds remaining.

Something Alex's dad had once said floated back to the top of her brain.

In sports, there wasn't just one way to keep score.

If they could come all the way back from being down 3–0, a tie would feel like a win today.

Whatever happens, Alex thought, *we're a team now.*

She felt fresher and faster in her last minute out there than she had in her first.

We just need one goal.

The Lions had taken some time off the clock, controlling the ball on their end. Alex couldn't tell how much, but she knew they only had moments to catch up.

She watched as Annie moved up to meet Adella, trying to slow her down, as Adella crossed into the Owls' end of the field.

Alex could either double-team her and force her to pass or attempt to guess her next move, which was near impossible for someone with seemingly limitless range . . .

Alex took a chance, though, and guessed that she would pass.

She felt like a defensive back in football, trying to read Adella's eyes, choosing to drop back into coverage.

Sure enough, Adella went for a long pass.

Alex stepped in at the last second to cut it off.

Defense into offense.

Just like that, she was running up the field at full speed, heading toward Palmer's goalie.

She took the middle of the field. Annie faded off to her right, Roisin still on the left. They were in perfect alignment, like a flock of geese in the sky.

Alex got past one defender.

Then another.

She saw a streak to her right, Adella getting back into the play, almost caught up with Alex.

Alex tapped into one last gear she didn't know she had.

With a quick glance, she spotted Annie, open to her right.

Alex didn't hesitate. With the Palmer keeper still focused on her, she push-passed the ball over to Annie, who was faced with a ton of empty net to the keeper's left.

Annie took a much bigger swing with her leg than she needed and nearly missed the goal wide right.

For a split second, Alex, from her angle, thought it *was* wide right.

It wasn't.

The ball clipped the post, but only a little, giving the keeper time to dive and nearly get a piece of Annie's shot.

The ball was just inches out of her reach, though.

Owls 4, Lions 4 at the final whistle.

27

LINDSEY DECIDED TO HOST A TEAM MEETING AT HER HOUSE THAT Saturday afternoon to discuss fundraising ideas. It was all hypothetical, of course. Coach Cross hadn't heard about approvals yet, and the idea of a boys vs. girls scrimmage hadn't even made it as far as the boys' coach. But the girls were confident and wanted to be prepared from the moment they got the green light.

Over the phone, Alex's mom asked if she could attend. She'd participated in a few recent 5K runs to benefit various nonprofits and knew a thing or two about raising money.

"I don't want to miss out on all the fun," Liza said.

It was a small gesture, but one Alex couldn't help but be moved by. Her mom. Coming to a soccer meeting. Like everyone else's parents. As if she'd been here all along.

The whole idea of it made Alex warm all over.

"Who said any of this is going to be fun?" Alex said. "Besides, we don't even know if we can pull it off."

"My money's on you, kid," her mom said, then told her she'd pick her up a little before three.

When Alex hung up, she called Gabe and asked if he was up for some light tossing in the backyard.

"I don't know, Alex," he said. "Don't think I'm ready for that."

It had already been over a week, and Dr. Calabrese had cleared Gabe for light exercise.

"Come on," Alex said. "I've been walking up and down the halls with you every day. You're due for a little football action."

"You know what they say," Gabe said. "Fake it till you make it."

"You don't have to run," Alex said. "You don't even have to move around. We'll just throw a ball back and forth like we've done a million times."

"When I didn't have a bad knee," Gabe reminded her.

"It's not a bad knee," Alex said. "It just misbehaved that one time."

"Maybe in a few days."

"Gabe," Alex said, leveling with him. "When your left knee is ready for baseball, which it's going to be, your right arm needs to be ready too."

"I just don't want to rush things," Gabe said.

"I talked to my mom," Alex said. "She basically said that if you can walk, you can throw."

Alex paused.

"You'd be doing me a favor," she said. "I need someone to help break in my new catcher's mitt!"

"Oh, so suddenly you're a baseball player, huh?" he joked.

"Well, *some*body needs to keep up with you."

"I assume you won't take no for an answer?"

"Bingo."

His mom dropped him off a half hour later. He wasn't ready to start riding his bike just yet, even though Dr. Calabrese and

Liza had told him that riding a real bike was as good for his knee as riding an exercise bike.

Alex knew what was going on. Gabe had never gotten seriously injured playing sports. A few times he'd gotten banged up in football, having to limp off the field. But that sort of thing happened to everybody. This was different. Gabe had told Alex—on more than one occasion—that he was afraid of getting hurt playing baseball, because that would mean having to forfeit football season. The fear of needing surgery paralyzed him. Suddenly the boy who always expected the best was now fearful of the worst.

Alex kept telling him that he was making too much of it. That he was a rock star when it came to sports, and he would rock rehab just the same.

But always, he'd have the same response for her: "It's not *your* knee."

This always made Alex feel a little queasy. The guilt would come flooding back, and she couldn't help but wish that it had been her knee instead of Gabe's.

Trying to shake the thought from her head, she concentrated on them being together in the backyard again, like old times.

"You really haven't thrown yet?" Alex asked as they walked out onto the grass.

"By myself," he said, "in my yard, using a bounce-back net. But even then, I forgot my knee and reached for a ball that'd bounced to my left. Felt a twinge or something, like I'd put too much weight on it."

"I won't make you reach," Alex promised. "You may remember

from football that I have a rather accurate arm."

That at least got a smirk out of him.

"Hard to forget," Gabe said.

He hadn't been wearing his brace at school the past few days, complaining that it itched, and he really didn't need it anyway.

But he was wearing it now.

"We'll stick to baseball today," Alex said. "I promise."

He had carefully paced off sixty feet between them, the distance between the pitcher's mound and home plate. It was technically sixty feet six inches, Gabe said, but neither one of them was going to be able to tell the difference.

At first, they just soft-tossed, Gabe barely striding at all with his left leg as his arm came forward, the way he would if he were pitching for real.

"Don't you put more strain on your arm when you don't use your legs?" Alex asked.

"Now you're an expert on pitching?" he said, half in jest.

"Ouch."

"Hey, if I've got a sprained knee, you can have a bruised ego."

"Touché."

"And now she's a fencer," Gabe said, throwing his hands to the sky.

Eventually, as he loosened up, he began to stride normally and throw the ball harder. Alex watched him and realized what a great quarterback he would have made if that were his ambition. But he'd always wanted to be a receiver.

Catching in one sport and throwing in another. The perfect balance.

Baseball had never been Alex's game. But she loved being out here with him, getting into a catcher's crouch and using her mitt to give Gabe a target, even calling out balls and strikes.

One time when she called a ball, Gabe said, "I want a new home plate umpire."

"Boo-hoo," Alex said. "The complaint department is closed."

"So that's the way it's going to be?"

"Don't make me throw you out of this game, young man," Alex said with pretend authority.

Before they'd started, Gabe said he only wanted to throw about fifty pitches total. But the more he got into it, the more Alex knew that promise wouldn't hold.

He threw harder now, the ball coming to Alex at top speeds. The pocket of the mitt popped with each catch.

She didn't ask him if he was glad he'd come, because it was obvious by the look on his face.

"One more batter and then we're done," Gabe called to her.

"Deal," Alex said.

"Get ready," he said. "Gonna bring it."

He burned one in for strike one. Alex didn't even have to move her mitt.

Did the same for strike two.

He's ready for baseball, Alex thought. *Even if he won't admit it.*

When he reached back to give it something extra for strike three, his left foot slipped on the grass.

He went down.

Hard.

The memories of his fall on the soccer field came back in a rush as Alex ran for him.

What would happen if he'd hurt himself again? Or made the injury worse? She'd been the one who'd invited him here to throw. It would be her fault . . . again.

She crouched down at his side and saw his hand reach for his knee.

"Are you okay?" Alex asked, hoping beyond hope that he'd say yes. That it was nothing.

But that's not what he said.

IT TURNED OUT ALEX'S MOM WAS ALREADY ON HER WAY TO THE house, as she and Jack were scheduled to have lunch together. Alex thought it was like having an orthopedic surgeon who makes house calls.

She had Gabe lean on her as they came inside, even though he insisted he was fine on his own.

"Not doing so good in your yard lately," he said in her ear.

Alex had never been happier to see her mom. Liza had Gabe sit on the couch and rest his leg on the ottoman in the living room. Then she spoke to him softly, as she had him make small movements with his leg.

"Does that hurt?" she'd ask. "How about this? Feel anything when you do that?"

"The only time it really hurt was when I landed funny," Gabe said. "Except it wasn't funny when it happened."

She had him do minor leg lifts then, one after another. Finally, she asked him to stand and put as much weight as he could on his left leg.

"Not bad, right?" Liza said.

"No," Gabe said, then looked at her quizzically. "But the way you say it makes it sound like you knew it wouldn't be."

She smiled at Gabe. "I've got a terrible poker face," she said.

"What happened today—not the slip, but the way you felt afterward—is just a normal part of recovery. What you probably felt was nothing more than scar tissue trying to heal up."

"But how do I know my knee isn't going to feel like that every time I pitch?" Gabe asked, a note of concern in his voice.

"It won't," she said. "I'm not comparing what happened to you to a muscle pull, Gabe. A sprain is technically more severe. But after people have pulled muscles, they think that area of their body will never go back to normal. But it always does."

He sat back down.

"How am I going to play if every time I'm going to be afraid of hurting my knee again?" he said.

"I can't tell you what to be afraid of," she said. "It's your knee, your body. But Alex told me about the way you were throwing today. Fearlessly. Without giving your knee a second thought. So if you ask me, what happened today was nothing more than a speed bump, and you're totally on track to start the season on time."

"Sure," he said, without much conviction.

He's hearing her, Alex thought. *But he's not believing her.*

Alex asked him if he wanted to stay for lunch, but Gabe politely declined, saying he just wanted to get home and relax. Alex's mom offered to drive him, and though he was grateful, he said he'd call his mom to come.

Mrs. Hildreth pulled up a few minutes later, and Alex walked Gabe out to the car.

"This is my fault," she said, hanging her head. "Again."

Gabe was quiet for a minute. Almost like maybe this time he

agreed with her. But then he said, "Nah, you didn't trip me. I just went a little too hard on that last pitch is all."

"Yeah, but I pushed you to come over," she said. "I encouraged it."

"I'll be fine," he assured her. "Seriously."

Now Alex was the one hearing but not believing him.

She watched her friend head toward his mom's car, limping slightly.

He opened the back seat door, then turned toward Alex. "Maybe the best thing for me to do is just bag baseball this season," he said.

Then he was in the car and gone.

"HE JUST NEEDS TO WORK THROUGH THIS ON HIS OWN," ALEX'S mom said on their way to Lindsey's house for the team meeting.

"What he's really afraid of is that he might miss out on two seasons because of this," Alex said. "Can't say I blame him."

"He's not going to miss out on anything," her mom said.

"How can you be so sure?"

"Because I've seen his sort of sprain a million and one times," she said. "Gabe's being cautious now, and that's okay. He's allowed to be scared. There's no shame in that."

They were at a stoplight, so she looked up at Alex in the rearview mirror and winked. "Even for tough ones like you and Gabe."

The Stiles house had a large living room, one that opened into their dining room and kitchen. Most of the parents sat at the dining room table, while the kids took spots on the floor or the L-shaped couch.

Alex had come up with a nickname in her head for what they were here to talk about:

SOS.

Save Our Season.

Lindsey was the first to get up and call the meeting to order. "So, we're all here to come up with some fundraising ideas," she started. "And everyone is encouraged to offer their suggestions."

She took a breath, then continued. "Carly's going to take notes on her laptop, so we can refer back to them as needed. No idea's a bad idea, but everyone should know that we obviously can't go with everyone's ideas. We'll have to agree on the best ones before moving forward."

Then Lindsey sat back down and gave Alex the floor.

Alex was a little caught off guard. She hadn't prepared to speak first, so she said the first thing that came to mind. "I've been calling our situation SOS," she said. "Save Our Season. Maybe that can be, like, our slogan or something?"

"SOS is a cool name," Annie said. "We should have T-shirts made."

"Oooh, T-shirts!" Maria said. "Everyone loves good swag."

"Mr. and Mrs. Banville have that T-shirt shop in town," Mrs. Stiles said. "I could call them up, see if we could get a good price."

"We could sell them at the game!" Afafa Agbayong said enthusiastically.

Rashida chimed in then. "What if it said BOYS VS. GIRLS, with just the date of the game underneath?"

"I think you mean GIRLS VS. BOYS," Carly said, grinning. "We get top billing."

"If the school gets behind this," Alex's mom said, "and you guys can get everybody fired up, those shirts could become collector's items, as long as they're not too expensive."

Roisin raised a hand.

"Before we go any further," she said, "can I ask about

something we haven't really discussed yet?" She looked around the room. "Exactly how much does a season cost?"

Alex had done some research online, but the numbers had varied for soccer teams across the state. She watched now as Coach Cross walked over and stood in front of the Stileses' picture window, facing everybody.

"I've actually talked to the school about the various expenses," she said, "as well as to our dear friends on the Town Council, to come up with a reasonable number."

She paused before breaking the news, "Twenty-five thousand dollars."

Alex thought the collective groan from her teammates might rattle the window right out of its frame.

"I know," she said. "It's a lot."

"A *lot*?" Maria said. "Twenty-five thousand may as well be twenty-five *million*."

"How are we going to raise *that* much money in only a few weeks?" Annie said.

Alex had been sitting on the love seat between Roisin and Lindsey. She found herself standing then and walking across the room to stand next to Coach Cross.

"We can do this," she said. "We can do this because we have to. Because we owe it to ourselves. We all saw what happened in that game against Palmer. We know how good we can be."

She wanted to draw Lindsey into this.

"Right, Lindsey?" she said.

Lindsey walked across the room now to stand next to Alex.

"We didn't give up against Palmer," Lindsey said. "We're not going to give up now before we've even begun, right?"

"*Right!*" was the shout from the room.

The next hour was spent brainstorming ideas. Maybe the best came from Alex's mom.

"We had to do something similar to this in high school once," she said. "There was this really popular assistant coach who was about to be let go from the football team. It was a budget thing. And you know what happened? The school rallied together and came up with the idea to print programs for the football games. We ran around town selling ads and eventually raised enough to save the coach's job."

"So we need to have a program for our game," Alex said definitively.

"It might turn out to be one of our biggest moneymakers," Coach said, "if the T-shirts aren't."

"Okay," Mrs. Stiles said. "What else?"

Then the ideas really started to fly.

Thinking of Sophie, Alex threw out the idea of a bake sale, and much to her surprise, the girls were totally into it. Roisin especially, who said it gave her an excuse to whip out her famous pound cake recipe.

Madison Antonino, one of the team's defenders, said they could raffle off a dinner at her family's restaurant in town.

Carly typed furiously, careful not to miss what anyone was saying.

"Dad and I have season tickets to the Steelers games," Alex said. "We can auction off a pair for one of the bigger games."

Now Afafa's hand shot up.

"We've got season tickets to the Pirates!" she said. "We can raffle those off too." She smiled, glad to be contributing to the cause.

The energy in the room was palpable. Ideas ricocheted off each other like the diagram of electrons in Alex's science textbook.

Carly said she had an uncle who worked at a well-known hat company and could maybe get them to donate some branded baseball caps. Ones that had THE GAME embroidered on them.

"By the way?" Alex's mom said. "Even though my daughter knows I'm not much of a sports expert, isn't 'The Game' what they call the Harvard-Yale football game every year?"

"Not in Orville, Pennsylvania, this spring," Alex said.

Before it was time to leave, they had broken the team up into various committees. One for the program and securing advertising, one for merchandise like T-shirts and hats, and one that covered raffles and the bake sale.

As they began to file out of the house, one of Alex's teammates started up a chant behind her.

"SOS . . . SOS . . . SOS!"

Everybody joined in. If they hadn't been a team before, they were now.

30

Until they got permission from the school and the Town Council, the team agreed they'd continue to keep The Game a secret.

"And once we do get approval, as I believe we will," Coach said, "we'll still need to get the boys on board."

Alex had been thinking that herself, even though Lindsey had made it seem as if the boys had no choice but to agree.

"Thing is," Coach said to Alex and her mom in Lindsey's driveway after the meeting let out, "the boys don't actually have anything to lose by playing. Only wounded pride, which to me is a small price to pay so that everyone can have a season."

"But that's just it, Coach," Alex said, "they don't have a season to lose. So playing isn't essential for them."

"Maybe so," Coach Cross said. "But if there's one thing you all have in common, it's a love of the game. It's not so easy to give up the chance to play when the opportunity arises."

She looked up at Alex's mom then, the two of them sharing a knowing glance, and Alex was pretty sure she knew what it was about.

Jack often spoke about how much he missed being out on the field as a kid, playing with his teammates. Those were some of the best times of his life. And from what Liza told Alex, not just about her own high school athletic experience but about Coach Cross's as well, they were both probably thinking how much they'd give for the opportunity to play again.

Alex hoped Coach Cross was right about the boys—that it wouldn't be an easy choice for them to turn down a game. But inside, she had her doubts.

Before practice on Monday afternoon, Coach sat the team down on the gym bleachers for an announcement. She seemed to be in high spirits, so the girls had every reason to believe there was good news coming their way.

And sure enough, there was. Coach had gotten a yes from the school to proceed with The Game. Not only that, but her old soccer buddy from high school, Mrs. McMahon, who sat on the Town Council, also approved the plan. They were as good as gold.

All that was left was for the boys to agree. Not just the players, but their coach, Mr. Selmani, as well. Coach Cross predicted Coach Selmani would probably leave it up to his players.

The girls' and boys' teams usually alternated between who got to use the practice field first. Lately, though, the boys had won out. The girls couldn't lay claim, seeing as their team wasn't legitimized by the school. Today the boys had it first, and the girls walked out together to meet them.

Coach Cross instructed the girls to start stretching while she went over and pulled Coach Selmani aside so the two of them could have a private conversation.

They were too far away to make out what was being said,

but Alex attempted to read their facial expressions and body language to get a sense of how Coach Selmani was reacting to the proposal.

To Alex, he seemed open to the idea. At least, he wasn't shaking his head no or anything.

When they were done, Coach Selmani waved his players over, and he and Coach Cross stood between the two teams.

Coach Selmani addressed the guys, explaining what the girls were hoping to accomplish with The Game.

"So what do you guys think about that?"

Chase Gwinn stepped forward, a spiteful grin spread across his face, as cocky as ever.

"Let me see if I have this straight," he said to Coach Selmani. "*They* want to challenge *us* to a game?"

Nobody on either team said anything right away, so Alex stepped forward.

"It's not like that," she said. "The challenge is for us to raise enough money so that we can have a season. We're putting together fundraising tactics is all."

"By putting us on the spot," he responded.

"By *playing* a game with you guys," Alex said. She could feel the frustration rising in her throat and told herself to cool off. They'd never agree to this if she lost her temper.

Chase held up a finger, as if telling Alex to wait, which Alex thought was completely rude.

"Let me talk this over with my boys," he said.

Like he owns the team.

Chase gathered his teammates around him. Alex couldn't

hear what he was saying. But the team meeting couldn't have lasted more than a couple of minutes.

"So we talked it over, and here's what we came up with," Chase said. "Let's do this right now. Our team against your, uh . . . non-team." That got a chuckle out of the boys. "Then we'll see if you can keep up with us enough in a real game."

"We're not trying to prove some point here," Annie said. "We just look at this as being a win-win for all of us."

"Yeah," Lindsey said. "Think of it as just another chance to play a game you enjoy in front of a crowd of people. Win or lose, it really doesn't matter."

"We *always* win," Chase said. "And win. And win."

Alex cracked a smile at him, even though she didn't mean it.

"In that case," Alex said, "*we* accept *your* challenge, as long as Coach Cross thinks it's okay."

Coach Cross grinned. "Fine with me," she said, looking toward Coach Selmani, who merely shrugged.

As both teams gathered together, Lindsey said to Chase, "The only thing you stand to lose, Gwinn, is the right to talk smack."

She wasn't as good a soccer player as Chase was, Alex thought. But if smack-talking were a sport, Lindsey would be second to none.

"You talk a big game, Stiles, but let's see if you can walk the walk," Chase said to her.

Lindsey glowered at him.

"I'm not the one who requested a practice scrimmage just to ensure I won't be embarrassed in front of a crowd."

Chase's face went beet red, and he opened his mouth to respond, but Coach Selmani cut him off.

"Okay, okay," he said, losing his patience a little. "We're about to have what's called a 'friendly' in soccer. So let's zip it on the chirping for the time being and play a thirty-minute half."

"It will serve as practice today for both teams," Coach Cross said.

Before very long—the first five minutes of play, in fact—the boys were already up by three goals.

Annie and Lindsey were no match for Chase and his two best strikers, Johnny Gallotta and Ryan Lazar. Even though it sometimes seemed as if Chase didn't need either one of them as his wingman. He was that kind of wizard with the ball, scoring the first two goals for the boys and making Carly look bad as she struggled to block them both.

Chase excessively celebrated both goals as if they were playing in the state championship and not just a practice scrimmage. The first time, he extended his arms out like an airplane and zoomed around the field, at one point getting up in Alex's face. On the next goal, he curtsied to Lindsey.

The second time, Coach Selmani yelled at him to cut it out.

Chase just laughed it off and ran back up the field as he and his teammates continued to dominate the first half.

He scored again a few minutes later, raising their lead to 4–0.

At that, Coach Cross blew her whistle and subbed in Alex, Roisin, Afafa, Rashida, and a few other new players.

At the next whistle, a couple of minutes later, Roisin sidled up to Alex and said, "Why do I feel like they're runnin' downhill while we're goin' uphill?"

"Just remember," Alex said to her, keeping her voice low. "This is *a* game. But it's not *the* game."

It was 7–0 by the time Coach Cross announced one minute left. By now Coach had switched Annie off Chase and stuck Alex on him. Even during play, he kept trying to chirp on her, but Alex ignored him. Or just laughed at his attempts to intimidate.

"You think this is funny?" Chase said.

"Well, Chase," she said, "I wouldn't give you a Netflix comedy special or anything, but it's fun to watch you try."

"Oh, I'm sorry," Chase said mockingly, "didn't realize the score was so amusing to you."

"Funny thing is," Alex said back, "you seem to be the only one concerned about it."

Alex could see how much Chase wanted to score again. The perfect cap to a perfect day. Showing up the girl he'd thought had claimed his rightly earned spotlight last fall.

He was sprinting up the field again, tongue out, like he did when he had full control of the play. Running directly at Alex, he faked a pass to Johnny, but Alex could see right through him.

She acted as if she'd bit on the fake, leaning Johnny's way, so that Chase thought he had a step on her.

He didn't.

Just as he started to blow past her, Alex went into a slide, knocking the ball away from him. It took Chase a moment to slow his momentum and turn back around. But by then, Alex had gotten to her feet.

Alex's ball now.

She made a quick pass to Roisin, who carried the ball into the boys' end. Chase wasn't going for her, though. He was trying to catch up with Alex.

He's fast, Alex thought.

But so am I.

Finding an extra kick of energy, Alex pushed herself into high gear, creating some room between herself and Chase. Then Roisin sent her the ball right back, and Alex gave a fast head fake to Justin Soares, the closest defender.

Then she was past Justin.

Alone against their goalkeeper, Danny Stroud.

Best keeper in the boys' league.

Alex didn't hesitate or try to get too fancy. She was counting on the fact that Danny believed she favored her right foot. Few knew that Alex was capable of using both.

As suspected, he guessed that she would hook one to his right. She didn't.

Instead, she slowed enough to fake a kick and pushed the ball behind her left foot.

And then absolutely flushed a shot into the top left corner.

Just like that, they were on the board.

It wasn't a total shutout.

Still a beatdown, by any measure, but they'd put up points, which was better than nothing.

Both coaches blew their whistles then, signaling the end of practice.

As the teams strolled off the field, no one dared say anything from either side.

Chase grinned smugly, but Alex was beginning to think that was his permanent expression.

As Alex and Roisin walked back toward the gym, Roisin said, "Might a girl ask why there's a big fat smile on your face after we just caught ourselves a beating like that?"

Alex took a swig from her water bottle and said, "Best loss I've ever had."

"And why is that?"

"Because now they think they can beat us like that in front of the whole town," Alex said.

Roisin looked confused. "Well, can't they?"

Alex took a breath. "Always a possibility," she said, "but their win accomplished two things today."

"Oh yeah?" Roisin said. "What's that?"

"One, they're confident enough to say yes to The Game, which is all we really needed anyway," Alex said. "And two? It got them thinking they've got this in the bag. Even though we hardly brought our A game today."

After the girls showered and dressed in the locker room, Coach Cross came in to deliver the good news.

Coach Selmani and the boys had agreed to play.

The Game was on.

Alex winked at Roisin. "Told ya."

31

COACH CROSS CUT THEM BACK TO FOUR PRACTICES A WEEK INSTEAD of their usual five.

On Fridays after school, they'd all meet in the gym to work on their respective projects for The Game.

Alex, Lindsey, and Roisin doubled down on developing the program. Alex's dad had hooked them up with a printer in town, and now they were focused on making a list of local businesses to approach for ads.

By now Annie and Rashida had made a huge breakthrough on T-shirts. Mr. and Mrs. Banville had offered them a rather large discount on a bulk order. They'd said they were happy to help, having both been Orville athletes themselves in their day. Now Annie and Rashida lay on the waxy gym floor, stomachs down, perusing the binders full of T-shirt colors, materials, logos, and text fonts for screen printing.

Carly's uncle was able to supply hats at a generous rate. Still, they'd need to sell enough to afford them, but if they charged a premium, her uncle said they'd be more than profitable.

Orville High had already allowed them to book its soccer field for the game, which meant plenty of seats in the bleachers. Alex's dad had a client with a small printing business—the same one they were using for the program—who agreed to help with the tickets to be sold on the day of the game.

Ally McGee and Maria Ochoa had set up a website with the help of Ms. Weiss, their computer science teacher. They had also created their own social media handles to start promoting The Game online and help generate early interest.

There was still a long way to go, but they could all feel things slowly coming together.

And while this kind of teamwork wasn't what Alex had in mind this season, it brought her closer to her teammates in unexpected ways. They were still aiming toward a goal, using their individual strengths, working together. But something about it felt even more fulfilling than being on the field.

They weren't just fighting for a win. They were fighting for a cause.

One of the most exciting things to come out of their efforts was that the *Orville Patch* had decided to run an article on The Game in one of their special weekly editions.

Lindsey was stoked. She said the exposure from the article alone was sure to draw crowds and maybe even get some businesses eager to purchase ads for their program or offer goods and experiences for the raffles.

The reporter writing the piece, Molly Cohen, had come to the middle school to interview Coach Cross. But Coach explained that the idea had been all Alex's and Lindsey's and invited them to her office so they could be quoted in the paper.

Per usual, Lindsey did most of the talking, but to Alex's surprise, she gave Alex credit for coming up with the initial idea to play the boys. This was new for Lindsey, Alex thought. Being gracious.

But it was Alex, at least according to her dad—hardly an impartial observer—who had the best quote in the story.

"We know how much money we need to raise," she told Molly Cohen. "But we can't put a dollar amount on how much this season would mean to us."

Lindsey, being Lindsey, had to add one final remark, which Molly used in the story: "This game is going to be the highlight of the season," she said. "You're not going to want to miss it."

Because journalists were supposed to be impartial, Molly had also included a quote from Chase.

When she'd asked him how the boys would react if the girls won the game, Chase said plainly, "They're not going to."

"But what if they do?" Molly pressed.

"They won't," Chase said.

The paper came out on Saturday afternoons. But the story about The Game was published in the digital edition late Saturday morning. Sophie had come over early in the afternoon so she and Alex could read it together on Alex's laptop.

"We won't know until The Game's over and we've counted up all the money if we've raised enough," Alex said when they finished reading. "Regardless of who wins or loses."

By now Sophie had thrown herself into practically every aspect of the project, as if she were an honorary member of the soccer team. She'd even come up with the design for the T-shirts, THE GAME on the front, a small illustration of a soccer ball underneath, with GIRLS VS. BOYS printed below.

The date of The Game would go on the backs of the shirts.

"But I know you, Alex Carlisle," Sophie said. "Even though the outcome of The Game won't affect the final score on the money, you want to beat them."

"I want people to see a good game," Alex said. "Mom says if we put on a show, people might buy even more merchandise on their way out."

They were lying against the pillows on Alex's bed, and Sophie gave Alex a playful shove into her favorite stuffed animal, Simba.

"That doesn't answer my question," Sophie said.

"I don't believe you asked me a question," Alex responded.

Sophie rolled her eyes. "Okay, then, here it is. How much *do* you want to beat Chase and the boys?"

"You know I do," Alex said. "But it's not the main thing on my mind. The object of this game is to make money."

"And maybe history!" Sophie said.

They scrolled through all the Instagram and Twitter posts about The Game. Ally had come up with the hashtag #OrvilleMiddleTheGame, which had generated the predictable trash talk between the students of Orville Middle. However, most of the posts were from people in town, showing their support and excitement for The Game.

"Did you have any idea it would be like this?" Sophie asked.

"Not a clue," Alex confessed.

"People are acting like it's some kind of soccer Super Bowl," Sophie said.

Worry started to spread across Alex's chest at Sophie's words. What if The Game didn't turn out to be all that exciting? What if the fans were disappointed in the performance? It wasn't like they were professionals out there. Was it unfair to charge people to watch a group of amateur players? She raised the issue with Sophie.

"I know I sound like I'm stuck on this," Alex said. "But I really do want the people to have a good time and get their money's worth. What if—"

"I'm gonna stop you right there," Sophie said. "First of all, The Game *will* be exciting, no question." She took a breath. "And also? You're not pocketing the money. You're using it to have the season you deserve. One you shouldn't have to fight for."

Alex nodded, supposing Sophie was right. "And if we *do* raise enough money," she said, "then our team can't lose, even if we have the lower score at the end of the night."

"But you don't want to lose to Chase Gwinn," Sophie said.

"Not even a little bit," Alex said, and laughed.

Sophie posted some funny comments about the boys on her Instagram stories. None of them mean, just trying to get them riled up. A few seconds later, the comments started flooding in. Some were snarky, as if the boys on the soccer team were trying to stick the needle in. But for the most part, everybody seemed to be getting into the spirit of what Alex thought The Game should be. A good old-fashioned rivalry. Like the Steelers versus the Ravens.

"You know what the very best part of all of this might be?" she said to Sophie.

"Being a part of a whole team of Billie Jean Kings?" Sophie guessed.

The girls had learned about Billie Jean King in their history class. A world-renowned female tennis professional who was a leader for equality in women's tennis and was still a prominent activist for women's rights today. The night before, they had streamed the *Battle of the Sexes* movie at Sophie's house. The story covered one of the most famous tennis matches ever played, where Billie Jean beat Bobby Riggs in a battle-of-the-sexes showdown. Emma Stone, one of Sophie's favorite actors, played Billie Jean.

"Ha!" Alex said. "As cool as it would be to win, that's not what I meant. The best part of this is getting to do something together with my mom."

"She's really into this, huh?"

"You *think*?" Alex said.

But it was in a good way. Alex and her mom had a deal. If Alex thought she was getting pushy, she was obligated to tell her.

"I don't want to be *that* mom," Liza had said.

The next day, Sunday, Alex's mom suggested Alex invite Roisin and Lindsey over to work on the program, and that she'd be around if they needed her.

The three girls gathered in Alex's living room and sprawled out with their notes and laptops.

Lindsey, who had a knack for digital design, took the lead on planning the layout with a program she had on her MacBook.

"We didn't have these resources when I was in school," Liza said. "I had to lay everything out on paper!"

"That sounds awful," Roisin said. "Genuinely awful."

"The real challenge will be selling the ads," Alex's mom said.

"But it's also the fun part. You get to go out in town, door to door. It's exciting!"

"Like a Girl Scout?" Alex said.

"What's a Girl Scout?" Roisin asked.

Alex realized they probably didn't have Girl Scouts in Ireland.

"It's like a youth organization that teaches girls life skills," Lindsey said. "Every year they go around selling delicious cookies, and everyone buys a million boxes apiece."

"I think my dad still has a few boxes of Thin Mints stashed away," Alex said. "But more to the point, I've never gone door to door selling anything before."

"It's like being a traveling salesman, except you won't have to leave Orville," Alex's mom explained.

"What's a traveling salesman?" Alex asked.

Her mom looked at her dad. They both smiled, almost sadly.

"Something old people know about," her mom said.

"I think the girls have it under control, Liza," Jack said. "Kids are a lot savvier now than we were at their age. With the googles and the snap-grams."

"Daaaad!" Alex moaned.

After a few hours designing the layout, Alex suggested they use the afternoon to hit the town and start filling up program pages. Among the three of them, and with some guidance from Liza, they came up with prices for full-page, half-page, and quarter-page advertisements. Coach Cross had printed out order slips for them to use with perforated receipts. It all seemed very official to Alex.

Lindsey suggested they start at Sam's, the pizzeria. "I always see their coupons in the pennysaver," she said. "They're pretty much guaranteed to take out an ad. Maybe two."

So Alex, Lindsey, and Roisin rode their bikes into town with their parents' permission, and sure enough, Sammy Jr., who managed the restaurant, agreed to a full-page ad on the spot. "Gives us an opportunity to promote our updated menu," he said. Then he gave each of the girls a "buy one slice, get one free" coupon, so they sat down to have lunch.

"Our first sale!" Roisin said. "They should all be as easy as this one."

"Well, I doubt that," Lindsey said, biting into her cheese slice, "but I'm still optimistic."

"Doesn't hurt to start off on the right foot," Alex added.

After lunch, they stopped at the paint-and-supplies shop, the corner pharmacy, Bostwick's ice cream, and plenty of other stores along the town's main street. Some people said yes. Others politely declined.

By four P.M., the girls had secured five spots in the program. Two of them full-page ads.

It was only their first attempt, but Roisin was fired up. "We crushed it!" she said as they walked back toward where they'd parked their bikes in front of Sam's.

"That we did," Lindsey said, "if I do say so myself."

"I don't know about you guys," Alex said, "but I'm delira and excira from just one afternoon of being in sales."

It was Irish slang that meant "delirious and excited."

"You looked that up!" Roisin said, slapping Alex lightly on the arm.

Alex grinned. "Maybe just a wee bit," she admitted.

Roisin laughed. "Yer deadly, you are."

The three of them mounted their bikes and rode home, splitting up at the end of the street to head toward their respective houses.

It had been a good day, and Alex was ready for the fun to continue. She and her dad had plans to whip up the Carlisle house specialty tonight for dinner: homemade thin-crust pizza.

But first, she ran upstairs to call Gabe and see how he was doing.

That turned out to be a mistake.

32

"Hey," she said, "I've got another hour before dinner. Can I come by for a bit?"

There was quiet on the other end. Then: "Kind of hanging with Jabril right now."

"Oh, okay," Alex said quietly. The three of them hanging out together had never been a problem before. She wasn't sure what provoked the change but decided not to press it.

There was a long pause then, as if they'd both already run out of things to say. Usually neither could get a word in edgewise on the phone, always talking over each other when they weren't finishing each other's sentences.

Except that wasn't the case just now.

"How's the knee?" she asked.

"You know you ask me how my knee is doing every single time we talk, right?" he snapped.

Alex was taken aback. "Because I genuinely want to know," she said.

"Even if I don't want to talk about it?"

Wow.

Alex knew he wasn't trying to be mean, but it sure sounded that way over the phone. Their friendship went back years— since elementary school. She cared about him and knew he cared about her too. But right now? This wasn't him.

This isn't us.

"Okay," she said again, at a loss for words.

She heard him sigh then. Loud enough she didn't need the phone to hear it. Probably could have opened her bedroom window and heard the sound carry all the way from Gabe's house.

"My knee is my knee," Gabe said. "I've been doing my exercises, but I've dialed them back a little."

Alex took a deep breath now. "You're not really thinking about bagging baseball, are you?"

"Yeah," he said. "I am." Like it was that easy.

"You can't," Alex pleaded. "You're too good."

"I know you're trying to be my friend," Gabe said. "But that's kind of my call and not yours."

Alex swallowed a lump in her throat. "But you were throwing the ball great the other day," she said in a small voice.

"It's not that big a deal!" Gabe shot back, his voice rising quickly. "It's just one season, and it's not even my favorite sport. If I'm not an idiot with my rehab"—he paused—"and I avoid things I shouldn't be doing, I could be good as new when football starts in August."

Alex could tell this wasn't the Gabe she knew. Because what he'd just said didn't line up at all with his philosophy on sports. He'd often told Alex that he'd never understood when kids their age chose to focus on only one sport. He thought they were missing out on way too much. Most especially getting to play with their friends.

But she wasn't about to bring that up now. *This isn't a debate,* she told herself.

She was sorry she had called.

"Hey," Gabe said. "Jabril is waiting to play video games."

Alex took the hint. "I guess I just . . ." She stopped. "I guess I just wanted to say that I'm sorry you got hurt."

Gabe almost seemed angrier now. "You need to stop apologizing," he said. "Nobody made me play soccer with you that day, and nobody forced me to play catch in your backyard."

"I feel like I made you," she said, now full of remorse.

Another silence then, longer than the one before.

"I want to help you get through this," she said. "It's the least I can do."

"I think you've done enough . . ." Gabe said.

As soon as the words were out of his mouth, though, Gabe tried to pull them back. "That came out wrong," he stumbled. "Now I'm the one who should be sorry."

"We both are," Alex said.

It was her last apology before the call ended. She had wanted to tell him everything that was happening with The Game. But now wasn't the time.

After a good day with her friends going door to door, now she felt as if one had just been slammed in her face.

THE TOWN OF ORVILLE BOASTED A NUMBER OF BEAUTIFUL community parks open to the public. The one Alex liked best wasn't the one closest to their house. But Alex's dad had taken her there when she was a little girl. It was called Montoya Park, and it wasn't so far away that she couldn't ride her bike there.

Monday was the coldest day they'd had in months, but Alex didn't care. After school let out and their practice ended, she bundled up in a hoodie and a sleeveless vest and headed over there with a soccer ball shoved in her backpack. She wanted to be alone. She wanted to run, she wanted to dribble, she wanted to kick the ball as far as it would go, retrieve it, then kick it again.

She wanted to restore all her positive feelings about The Game from the day before. Everything she'd felt going around town with Lindsey and Roisin. Alex had to laugh at the irony—wanting to reminisce about time spent with Lindsey Stiles. But it was true. What was the saying? Teamwork makes the dream work.

She wanted to trust that their hard work would amount to having a season, because if it did, it would be her greatest achievement to date. In sports and everything else. Or if not the greatest, then certainly in the top three. Bigger than a win. A significant moment Orville would always remember.

The park would also help take her mind off the conversation she'd had with Gabe. Alex tried to put herself in Gabe's shoes. It didn't matter how minor the injury was or that the doctors had cleared him to play. Only he knew how much he was hurting, and it wasn't Alex's place to tell him how to feel or what to do.

If he decided he didn't want to play baseball, well, then that was his decision, not hers.

When Alex grew tired of running around and taking out her frustration on the ball, she sat down on one of the swings.

And thought:

Things were a lot simpler when Dad used to take me here.

But now she remembered something her dad had once said. Something *his* father had told him about being a parent:

The bigger they get, the bigger the problems.

"Your dad told me I'd find you here," she heard.

She knew without looking that it was Jabril. Twisting herself around in the swing, she greeted him with a limp smile.

"I'd ask you to play," she said, touching the ball in her lap, "but you might get hurt."

Jabril shook his head. "I'd say you're right," he said, "but we both know I'm more of a superhero than Black Panther."

Jabril, Gabe, and Alex had seen the movie three times together when it had released in theaters. Gabe had said the test of a really good movie was if you were already thinking about seeing it again while the credits rolled. When the actor who'd played T'Challa, Chadwick Boseman, had died so young, they all felt as if they'd lost their hero.

"I would have called you last night," Jabril said, "but I ended up sleeping over at Gabe's."

Alex opened her mouth to speak, but Jabril held up a hand.

"And you don't have to tell me what happened, 'cause I heard every word."

"Not good, right?" Alex said.

"Not good and not Gabe," he said. "Just don't tell him that I said that."

He sat down on the swing next to hers. Jabril and Gabe were about the same height, average for seventh graders. But every other thing about Jabril was big. His heart, his smile, his talent, and his personality. He also played a big game, as a one-man wrecking crew at linebacker.

"He sounds really angry with me," Alex said. "I get it, though."

Jabril pushed back on the woodchips under his feet and began swinging back and forth. Then he pumped his legs to go higher. Alex laughed and told him to stop, afraid he might loop all the way over the set.

Finally, he slowed down. "He's not mad at you," he said. "At least I don't think so. He's just mad at the whole situation. He hates being hurt, and more than that, he hates being scared."

"I know," she said. "I just wish there was something I could do."

Jabril nodded. "On top of everything else, he knows the weather's about to get nicer—even if today's no indication—and everybody's going to be outside playing some kind of sport. That jams him up even more."

Alex leaned over, elbows to knees, and rested her head in her hands.

"Come on, Alex," Jabril said, trying to comfort her, "you gotta stop feeling guilty. What happened was *sports*. Nothing you did or didn't do."

"Yeah, but it never would have happened if I hadn't invited him to play."

"Yeah, so?" Jabril said. "You could say that about pretty much anything. If Terry Bradshaw's pass hadn't ricocheted off Jack Tatum's helmet, the Steelers would never have won the AFC Championship."

Jabril, of course, was referring to the Immaculate Reception, one of the most famous plays in NFL football.

Alex smirked. "Trying to appeal to the fan in me?"

"Think of it this way," Jabril said. "Say it's a football game and you throw one to your favorite receiver, over the middle. You lead him perfectly, but when he gets his hands on the ball, he bobbles it slightly and gets planted by some dude who's the Jabril of the other team. Now, is that your fault because you threw him the ball? Heck no. It's just *sports*. It's like my daddy says: you play the game, you take your chances."

"That's just it, though," Alex said. "One slip doesn't mean he's not getting better."

"See there, that's your problem," Jabril said. "You want this all to be logical and make sense. It doesn't matter what we think or what your mom or Dr. Calabrese says. It's what *he* thinks. And right now he thinks he's just gonna keep hurting it if he keeps playing."

"I've got to find a way to get him through this," Alex said.

Jabril smiled. "I know you're eager to make things better,

Alex. But sometimes the best way to help is to give him space and let him figure things out on his own."

"You know how hard that is for me!" Alex said.

"I do," he said. "Hard for me too. But not harder than it is to be Gabe right now."

Alex breathed in the cold afternoon air. "What if he really does decide to quit the baseball team?"

"Then there's nothing we can do about it," Jabril said. "All we can do is be the friends he needs us to be."

"It would be a lot easier if we were all on the same team like last fall," Alex sighed.

"The best thing you can do for now is focus on *your* team."

He pointed to her ball.

"So," he said, "think you could turn me into a soccer player?"

Alex chuckled. "You're not thinking of trying out for the team, are you?"

Jabril shook his head. "All I'm doing this spring is football training with some of the guys from the team. I stink at everything else."

"I'm sure that's not true," Alex said.

Then they both stood up and walked through the playground over to the grass that stretched all the way to the end of Montoya Park. Jabril put out his hand, and Alex tossed him the ball. He placed it on the grass, took a couple of steps back, swung his right leg, and sent the ball skidding into the dirt, several feet from where Alex was standing.

"Told you," he said. "Think I'll stick to football."

Alex peered over at Jabril and pursed her lips together into a tight smile. Her way of telling him she appreciated him coming out here. Talking to her. Making her feel better about the whole Gabe thing.

She had come out here for the purpose of clearing her head. Jabril did her one better. He lent her his ear and his advice. And for the first time in what felt like weeks, a weight lifted off her chest.

Finally, she could allow herself to feel excited about all there was to come and devote her full attention to The Game. Her whole body felt lighter, kicking the ball around with Jabril. Sports could make you glad that way.

But not always.

When they got to practice on Monday, Coach Selmani and the boys' team had some news.

34

CHASE GWINN HAD HURT HIS ANKLE THE DAY BEFORE, PLAYING A pickup game with some of his teammates on the fields at Orville Middle.

From what one of the girls on the team had heard, it was totally Chase's fault. It had gotten around that Chase was showing off his version of Pelé's signature bicycle kick.

Except he hadn't quite mastered it yet.

It was probably the most famous shot in the history of soccer. Pelé, with his back to the goal, kicked up from the ground and flipped backward, almost floating parallel to the ground as he somehow, magically, kicked the ball into the goal behind him.

Plenty of other soccer players had tried the move after him with varying degrees of success. Alex was skeptical of how many players had been able to pull it off in the seventh grade. But Chase was determined to show his buddies that he could do pretty much anything he wanted on a soccer field.

Unfortunately, this time, he couldn't.

He had landed awkwardly, ending up in so much pain that Dr. Calabrese feared it might be a *high* ankle sprain, the worst kind of ankle injury. One that could take up to two months to heal.

Chase hadn't shown up at school on Monday, and the doctors

wouldn't get the results of his MRI scan until Thursday or Friday at the earliest. Apparently, the lab was backed up this week. In other words, Chase wouldn't be as lucky as Gabe had been getting his results back.

Coach Cross told the girls all this while they were waiting to take the field for practice. The boys had the field first today. That's also when she told them there might be a problem with The Game.

"I hope it's not serious for Chase," Alex said. "My friend Gabe might be out a whole season, and he only suffered a minor sprain."

She didn't add that he probably didn't *have* to be out a whole season, but that was beside the point.

"What does Chase's injury have to do with our game, though?" Annie asked.

"Apparently," Coach Cross said, "the boys got together and decided that if Chase can't play, they don't want to either."

Alex's heart sank into her stomach.

"They can't do that!" Lindsey shouted, her voice bouncing off the gym walls.

"Don't they understand how much this game means to us?" Carly said.

"And how much work we've put into it?" Roisin said.

"I'm not sure they're thinking that way," Coach Cross said, playing devil's advocate. "Chase is their star player and lead scorer. They must feel as if their odds have gone down overnight."

"So you're saying they basically only want to show up if they're sure they can win?" Lindsey said.

"That's not exactly what they said to their coach," Coach Cross said. "They just feel as if their team isn't their team without Chase on it."

Alex could feel her face turning red. Her cheeks burning hotter by the second.

"People get hurt all the time in sports," she said, "and the games still go on."

"The boys aren't against having a game," Coach said, "they just want to delay it until Chase is better. Except—"

"Except if it's that high ankle thing," Lindsey interjected, "he could be out the whole season."

"Or," Coach Cross said, attempting to defuse the tension, "it could turn out to be just a mild sprain and he'll be back in a couple of weeks. Let's not jump to conclusions just yet."

Alex wasn't sure if her teammates had processed what Coach had said. But she had. And it sent her into a panic.

"We don't have a couple of weeks," she said. "In a couple of weeks, the season will have started. You said yourself the league's already waited as long as they can to fit us into the schedule."

"It's worse than that," Annie said, her voice full of disappointment. "I'm pretty sure the T-shirts have already been made, with the date of The Game on them. And if the hats aren't done yet, they're about to be."

Lindsey said, "And the program has to go off to the printer by this weekend."

A dark cloud settled over the gym.

"We can't start all over again," Alex said, choking down a frog in her throat.

The gym fell silent again. It was as if they'd rolled all the way back to the day the *Orville Patch* reported there wasn't going to be a seventh-grade girls' soccer season.

"What can we do?" Alex said to Coach Cross, hoping she'd have some miracle solution and they could all go home and pretend this never happened.

"Two things," Coach said, holding up her fingers. "One that will be easy, one not so easy."

"Tell us the easy one first," Alex said. "Think we could all use some good news today."

"We keep working," Coach said. "We keep working on and off the field as if The Game's going to be played as scheduled. We stick together as a team, which I *know* is easy for you guys."

"And the hard part?" Roisin asked.

Coach Cross sighed. "We wait."

35

CHASE DIDN'T RETURN TO SCHOOL UNTIL WEDNESDAY, WEARING A walking boot on his right ankle. Johnny Gallotta told Alex before their second-period earth science class that he was still waiting on his MRI results.

Between classes, Alex ran into Chase in the hallway and politely asked how he was doing.

Injury or no, he was still the same old Chase. "You concerned about me or about our game?"

Alex widened her eyes at him. "That's not fair," she said. "I don't like seeing anybody get hurt."

"If you want the truth," Chase said as he limped beside her, "I don't see any way I can play a soccer game in ten days."

"Is that what the doctor says?"

"It's what my *ankle* says," Chase said.

"Well," Alex replied, "I hope you feel better, whether you believe me or not."

With that, she headed down the hallway, toward English class. Chase went in the other direction.

"Hey," he called after her.

Alex stopped and turned around.

"This game was never that big a deal to me in the first place," he said.

"Never thought it was," Alex said. "But I assumed losing your entire season might be."

Then Chase was the one turning and heading for his next class. His limp, Alex thought, was a lot more pronounced than when she'd seen him walking into school that morning, as if it were put on for Alex's benefit.

Later, Alex was eating lunch with Roisin and Annie when she saw Chase sit down next to Gabe in the cafeteria. Alex couldn't believe it. As nice as Gabe was, she knew he had no use for Chase. Like pretty much everyone in their grade, Gabe saw Chase as being a conceited jerk.

"This isn't good," Alex said.

"What?" Roisin said. "The mac and cheese?"

Alex nodded discreetly in the direction of Gabe and Chase.

"What's the matter with them having lunch together?" Annie asked.

"It's not that," Alex said. "Just don't think Gabe is the best person for Chase to be talking to right now."

"Why not?" Roisin asked.

"Between us? Gabe doesn't think his knee is getting better," Alex said. "Even though my mom—a pediatric surgeon—pretty much told me he's almost fully healed. He's ready to throw his entire pitching season away because of it."

"And he's using his knee as an excuse not to play?" Roisin said.

"Not an excuse," Alex said. "A reason."

Roisin cocked her head, not comprehending.

"With Gabe there's a difference," Alex explained. "He never makes excuses for anything."

She kept sneaking glances across the room. At one point she saw Chase shove out from his seat and put all his weight on his injured leg. Gabe got up and did the same, demonstrating the weakness there. Then they both shook their heads and sat back down.

"We need Chase to get his MRI results back," Annie said.

"Waiting is total bruscar," Roisin said.

When Alex and Annie looked at her curiously, she translated, "Rubbish."

"What bothers me the most," Alex said, "is that The Game shouldn't depend on whether Chase can play. He's far from my favorite person, but I don't think it's fair to put all the pressure on him either. We're not playing Chase Gwinn in a game. We're playing the entire seventh-grade boys' team. They're just choosing to let Chase's injury stop them from participating."

There was nothing Annie or Roisin could say to that, so they just nodded and finished their lunches. Silently, they all agreed, this was a sticky situation.

The bell rang then, and Alex watched as Gabe and Chase got up from their table, both pouring it on thick with their heavy limps.

"That's not lookin' good for us," Roisin said.

They watched as Gabe and Chase slowly made their way out of the cafeteria.

"I never thought I'd hear myself say this," Annie said, "but I'm rooting for Chase Gwinn."

ON THURSDAY NIGHT, THE TEAM RECEIVED AN EMAIL FROM COACH Cross that Chase's MRI results came back showing no signs of any real damage. She'd heard from Coach Selmani that Chase's ankle was definitely swollen and bruised and that Dr. Calabrese advised icing it every day and keeping it wrapped and elevated as often as possible.

But Coach Cross also pointed out that when she'd asked Coach Selmani if that meant The Game was back on, he said it would still be up to the team at large.

Coach said she'd told Coach Selmani that postponing The Game at this point wasn't an option and that he understood the circumstances and said they'd talk again on Monday.

"So we have to wait a little more?" Alex said to Coach before their practice on Friday. Coach Selmani had given the boys the day off, and though ordinarily the girls took Fridays to work on The Game, they couldn't pass up an empty field.

"This is the worst," Lindsey said. "It's like Chase gets to decide our entire season."

"It's not just him," Alex reminded everyone. "It's the other guys who voted not to play without him."

When it came down to it, though, Alex didn't know which would be easier: convincing one person to play or convincing an entire team to play without their star player.

She and Chase may not have had much in common, but they were both passionate about their sport. Sure, Chase tried to act like missing The Game was no big deal, but Alex knew it was cutting him deep. For someone who loved to show off, he was giving up an incredible opportunity to do it in front of the whole town.

She kept coming back to that. To her hope that Chase's pride would win out.

"I still think he's looking for an excuse to cancel The Game," Annie said.

"Remember when I sprained an ankle last season?" Carly said. "Right at the end of a game. And I was back in there the next Saturday."

Surprisingly, Alex found herself jumping to Chase's defense. "Everybody's injuries are different," she said.

After talking to Jabril earlier that week, Alex realized it was unfair to expect other people to share her perspective. Had their circumstances been reversed, and Alex was the one injured, who's to say she wouldn't have felt just as Gabe or Chase did now? Would she be worried about next year's football season? Would she hesitate to play because of the risk she might injure herself worse? From the outside, it appeared as though they were milking their injuries, and maybe they were. But that wasn't Alex's call. In both cases, it came down to how comfortable the person was playing. Even if they were fully healed.

"Well, just because he has one shouldn't mean everything we've done should go to waste," Lindsey said. Then she crouched down in the grass and grabbed both sides of her head. "Gah! I hate waiting!"

"Pretty sure nobody likes it, Linds," Roisin said, stretching her hamstring.

"Waiting is fine, but there's gotta be something we can do in the meantime," Annie said.

That night, Alex came up with something.

Two things, actually.

37

ELEVEN THIRTY SATURDAY MORNING, ALEX PAID GABE A SURPRISE visit at his house.

When he opened the door and saw her standing there, he said, "You could've called first. It's not like I would've told you not to come."

"But you might have," Alex said, pressing her lips together in a tight grin.

"Well," Gabe said, "you got me there."

Alex caught a hint of a smile on his face.

A good sign.

A good start, anyway.

"Don't tell me," he said. "You're here because you want to help me."

"Nope," Alex said, "I'm here because I want *you* to help *me*."

They went inside. Gabe said his parents were at their favorite place: the home-improvement store.

"What are they looking for?" Alex said.

"See, that's the thing with them," Gabe said. "Most of the time they don't know until they get there."

They sat in the living room, because Gabe insisted Alex did *not* want to see the current state of his bedroom. His mom had threatened to hide his Xbox controller if it wasn't cleaned by the end of the day.

Alex had rehearsed what she would say to Gabe on the way over. She wasn't here to ask him about his knee. She wasn't going to pry about whether he'd decided to quit baseball. And she totally wasn't going to worry about him getting angry with her.

"Sometimes," Jack had said before she left the house, "friends have to tell each other things they don't want to hear."

"So, what's up?" Gabe said. "You have that look."

Clearly Alex had to work on her poker face. Between Gabe and her dad, they could read her like a book.

Alex inhaled deeply. "So, I know it's a personal decision. And I'm not here to force you to do anything," she began, "but as your friend, I need to say this."

Gabe looked at her expectantly.

"If the doctor clears you for baseball," Alex said, "I think you should play."

Boom.

There it was.

"Really . . ." Gabe said, but Alex cut him off.

"I'm sorry you got hurt," Alex kept on, "and then re-hurt or whatever. You know I blame myself. We don't need to talk about it, because you've heard me say it a dozen times." She stopped to take in some air. "But you're not the first person to get hurt, Gabe. And if you don't play, I think you'll regret it."

This wasn't all of what she'd planned to say.

But it was most of it.

When she finished Gabe said, "Can I say something now?"

He waited. She waited. He was on the couch, his left leg perched on the Hildreths' coffee table. Alex sat in a chair across from him, leaning forward.

"Let me just say one more thing," Alex said.

"Is there any way I can stop you?"

"You could try," she said, then plowed ahead.

"The baseball team starts practicing outside this week," she said. "You could be out there with them. And if you want to get extra throws in or whatever, I'm here for you. I'll do whatever it takes."

Gabe held back a smile, and Alex had to admit, that wasn't the reaction she'd expected from him. Anger? Yes. Denial? Absolutely. But now Gabe looked as if someone had told a joke in class and he was choking back laughter.

"*Now* may I say something?"

"Go ahead," Alex said, leaning back in her chair.

"I just came from seeing Dr. Calabrese," he said. "He cleared me to play. And I'm going to play. And unless something awful happens before then, I plan to be pitching next Friday."

Alex's mouth went slack. "Seriously?!" she said. "You let me give that whole speech even though I didn't have to?"

"I kind of enjoyed it," Gabe said, grinning. "And I could tell it meant a lot to you."

Alex got up and messed up his hair, like she sometimes did. "You couldn't have told me when I got here?"

"You barely gave me the chance!"

Alex had to admit he was right, but still. "Did your knee injury affect your texting ability?"

"You know I would have given you the good news," Gabe said. "I literally just got home ten minutes before you arrived."

"Fine, fine," Alex said. Then: "Sooooo, you wanna play catch?"

There was no use beating around the bush.

Now Gabe really smiled. A big one. Big as he had. The old Gabe now, 100 percent.

"You brought your mitt?" he said.

"Maybe . . ."

He told her to meet him in his backyard. He had to change into sneakers and grab his ball and glove from the garage.

Halfway up the steps, though, he stopped. "Wait a minute," he said. "You said you came over because you wanted my help."

"Tell you outside," she said.

Once she did, he asked, "You really think this will work?"

"Why not?" Alex said. "I'm on a roll."

Alex wasn't sure if her roll was going to continue. But by the next afternoon, the girls on the soccer team, with Mrs. Hildreth's permission, had turned the Hildreth living room into their office. Alex and Liza went over together.

Annie and Carly were counting up T-shirts now, separating them into piles of smalls, mediums, larges, and extra-larges. On Saturday, a bunch of Alex's teammates had gone back into town and sold more ads, which meant more pages to lay out before all the copy for the program went to the printer.

They still didn't know what was going to happen with Chase or with the boys. But they proceeded as if The Game was still on for next Saturday. Their energy and enthusiasm never wavered.

Every girl on the team was there except for Rashida, who'd come down with a case of strep throat. Unfortunately, her doctor said she'd be out for at least a week, meaning she'd have to miss The Game, if it took place.

Sophie had also come over to help, and about a half hour after most of the team had arrived, the doorbell rang and there was Jabril, standing on the other side of the door.

"It would have been like having a party and not inviting him," Gabe explained when he noticed Alex's shocked yet delighted expression.

"And *that*," Jabril said, "would have been a tragedy."

"If you're going to be here, though," Alex said, "you have to contribute somehow."

"Alex . . ." he said. "You know nobody in our school is better at getting the word out than I am."

"You mean the word about our game?" Lindsey said.

"The word about anything!" Jabril said.

Alex looked around the room. There were six laptops going at once. Mrs. Hildreth was helping with the page layouts, having once worked on her college yearbook. She and Alex's mom, with Lindsey and Roisin, were all hovering over Lindsey's laptop.

At one point Alex's mom looked around the room, smiled, and said, "Organized chaos has never looked so good."

Then Gabe's mom said, "I'm still not sure how our house turned into headquarters today, not that I mind."

"You'll see," Alex said. "And thank you again, Mrs. Hildreth. Really appreciate you letting us take over your living room for the day."

"Don't mention it!" Gabe's mom said. "I haven't had this much fun since planning Gabe's first birthday party."

"Mom," Gabe droned. "Shall we not?"

They were just finishing their break for cookies and lemonade when the doorbell rang again. Alex and Gabe jumped at the exact same moment and yelled, "I'll get it!"

Gabe had the honor of opening the door.

On the other side was Chase Gwinn.

He looked at Gabe, then Alex, then past them and into the living room, as if he'd just been ambushed.

"We need to talk," Alex said to him.

No one had moved from the doorway.

"You didn't tell me they would all be here," Chase said to Gabe, like Gabe had fooled him into coming.

"Well, yeah," Gabe said. "But I didn't tell you they wouldn't be here either."

Alex glanced down. She noticed that Chase was no longer wearing his walking boot.

"I'll . . . we . . . we can do this another time," Chase said, turning to go.

"No," Gabe said, reaching out to put a hand on Chase's shoulder. "You should stay."

"What's going on here?" Chase said.

He stepped inside now, and Gabe closed the door behind him, as if afraid Chase might try to escape.

"We're trying to have a season," Alex said. "I just thought you should see what that looks like."

"What's this got to do with me?" Chase said.

"Pretty much everything, dude," Gabe said quietly.

The girls looked up from their work and shouted greetings at Chase. Even Lindsey acted as if she were happy to see him, which Alex thought was quite possibly the best acting job Lindsey Stiles had ever pulled off.

Alex's mom came over carrying a tray of Mrs. Hildreth's homemade cookies. Chase reluctantly took one.

"Alex told me you didn't sustain a high ankle sprain," Alex's mom said. "That's wonderful news."

Chase looked confused, so Alex told him, "My mom's a specialist in sprained ankles."

Liza chuckled. "That's my daughter's way of describing my medical career."

"Well, I mean, yeah, she does other stuff too."

"So how is it feeling today?" Liza asked Chase.

Chase shrugged. "Still in pain."

"But you're not wearing your walking boot," she said. "So it can't be hurting too badly."

"But it still hurts," Chase said.

She smiled. "I'm sure it does." She walked back into the kitchen then, to chat with Gabe's mom.

Ally and Maria were sitting cross-legged in the corner of the living room with their phones out. Today's social media strategy was to post "fun facts" about as many of the girls on the team as possible. Anything to get people talking about The Game.

Alex took Chase on a tour around the room, explaining what everybody was doing, even though he hadn't asked.

I've never seen him this uncomfortable in his life, Alex thought.

"This is all about one soccer game?" he said, looking at Alex.

"If there is one," Alex said, hoping she'd opened his eyes to their dilemma.

She walked into the room and grabbed a couple of printouts so he could see what the T-shirts were going to look like.

"Cool," Chase said, not knowing what else to say.

"But what would be totally *uncool*," Gabe said, "is if they were doing all this for nothing."

Chase gestured to him and Jabril. "What do you guys have to do with The Game?"

"We're honorary team members," Gabe said. "Just doing what we can to help out."

"But you're guys," Chase said. "And you don't even play soccer."

"Does that matter?" Jabril said. "It's not about personal gain. It's about the larger cause."

Chase stared at him, still a little hesitant.

Then he turned to Alex. "You said you wanted to talk."

Gabe led them into the kitchen. Chase and Gabe sat down at the kitchen table, but Alex remained standing. Even when she had to present to the class, she couldn't simply stand in front of a podium. She had to be in constant motion. Like she was giving her own TED Talk.

Before she could say anything, Chase blurted, "This game isn't all on me, if that's what this is all about. And it's not as if I asked to get hurt."

Alex shook her head. "I'm not here to accuse you of anything, Chase," she said. "And you're right—it's not your fault you got hurt, and The Game shouldn't depend on you alone."

Chase looked to Alex as if to say: *Then what am I doing here?*

Alex took her cue to continue. "Problem is, all the other guys on your team say they won't play if you don't."

"I didn't tell them to do that," Chase rushed to say. "Johnny said we should vote on it, and we did. My vote didn't count more than anybody else's."

"You may not think so," Gabe said, "but a team looks to their leader for direction. So you voting no sent a powerful message to your boys. They followed your lead."

Alex could see what Gabe was doing. Appealing to Chase's ego to get him to come around. Like reverse psychology. By Gabe acknowledging how much influence Chase had over his team, it might get Chase to change his mind about The Game.

"I still don't know what you want me to do," Chase said.

"Listen," Gabe said. "I get it. I got hurt too, and it's not fun. Even when the doctors tell you it's fine, there's still a part of you that worries it might be worse than they're telling you."

Chase was paying attention now.

"I got so anxious worrying about my knee that my brain got twisted all around. I thought it'd never heal and started telling myself that baseball was out of the question. But once I started listening to the doctors and getting back out there, I realized it was all in my head."

Chase was quiet for a minute. Then he spoke. "If I'm ready, I'll play," he said. "I just don't know if I'll be ready in time."

"We obviously can't make you do anything," Alex said. "But if you can't be a leader on the field, could you at least be one off it?"

"Not sure I'm following . . ."

"You see what we're doing here," Alex said, gesturing toward the living room. "You see how much effort we're throwing into this game. If you can't play on the day, at least convince your teammates to take the field without you."

After another beat, Chase stood up, said he was leaving, and walked out of the kitchen.

"Wait," Gabe said, jogging to catch up with him. "Got time for a short walk? We'll go slow. Me with my knee. You with your ankle. Just down the street and back."

Chase hesitated, but finally said, "Okay. But then I have to bounce."

For a short walk, Alex thought they were gone a long time.

When Gabe returned, he was alone. He came through the back door, into the kitchen, where Alex was waiting for him.

Gabe stood there, arms crossed in front of him, shaking his head.

"What?"

Then Gabe grinned.

"Guess who else got cleared to play without telling us?" Gabe said.

"You're joking."

"Nope," Gabe said. "Our new bud Chase failed to mention that Dr. Calabrese gave him the thumbs-up a few days ago."

Gabe said that Chase still wouldn't commit to playing on game day. Just to practicing again by Tuesday. Wednesday at the latest.

"Fact is," Gabe said, "he wants to get back on that field as much as anyone. If for no other reason than that he misses playing. He doesn't want to give up one game, even if it isn't a league game."

"Now he knows how we feel," Alex said.

Alex reminded Gabe that payment was due for the T-shirts

and hats, and they needed to get the program copy to the printer tomorrow.

"You can go ahead," Gabe said. "He may not have confirmed it, but he's going to play."

Alex bumped him some fist.

"Chase said one last thing before he left," Gabe said. "It was some chirp, actually."

"Directed at me?"

"Who else?"

Alex waited to hear what words of wisdom Chase had decided to grace her with today.

"He said to tell you that now he wants to bury you guys."

"Ha!" Alex laughed.

Then she said, "Bring it."

As the excitement for The Game was building, word around school was that Chase would return to practice on Wednesday. But he was out there on Tuesday instead.

Coincidentally, Tuesday was the same day the hats were delivered. The programs were scheduled to arrive that Thursday, and the plan was to set up a table outside the cafeteria with shirts and hats for sale. They were also holding back enough inventory to sell at The Game on Saturday.

So the good news for the moment wasn't just that Chase was back on the field and The Game was officially on, but also that the money was starting to come in from sales of the merchandise. The town came through, and small businesses had generously bought up ads for the program. Orville's main grocery store had agreed to provide drinks for the concession stands and said the profit would go straight to the girls. Rocky's Hardware had stepped up and written them a very nice check to secure the one-day-only naming rights for the soccer field at Orville High.

Adding up what they'd made so far through ads and presales, they estimated they'd have to sell $5,000 worth of shirts and hats between now and Saturday to make their number.

That's what Coach told them before practice on Wednesday afternoon.

"Let me worry about the bottom line for the rest of the week," Coach said. "I want you guys to focus on The Game."

"But the money is the most important thing *about* our game," Lindsey said.

Coach shook her head.

"You can't put a price tag on a game you're going to remember for the rest of your lives," she said.

"They think we don't stand a chance," Roisin said.

"That's what the boys have been saying all over school," Annie said. "That they're going to clobber us worse than they did during our scrimmage."

"Perfect," Alex said. "That's just what we want them to think."

They were scrimmaging every day now in preparation for the weekend. On Wednesday, Annie finally won for her side with the prettiest goal Alex had seen from her since they'd started practicing. It was with her left foot, which by now was almost as good as her right, and the shot was from at least twenty yards away from Carly. Didn't matter. The ball ended up in the upper corner, and there was nothing Carly, as athletic as she was, could do about it. A bomb. Everybody on the field stopped and applauded.

Without anybody having to say a word, there was a universal feeling permeating the group. Each of them could feel it. They were as ready as they were going to be for Saturday's game.

Now all they had to do was wait until Saturday afternoon.

The girls had secured the soccer field first on Wednesday, and Gabe had practiced early with the baseball team, so his mom picked him and Alex up and drove them over to Alex's house for one last game of catch before he pitched against the Seneca Bears on Friday at an away game. The girls' soccer team planned to have a light workout that afternoon so they could reserve their energy for The Game on Saturday.

But for now, in her backyard, Gabe told Alex he wanted to have what the big-league pitchers called a "side session" to loosen up before playing the Bears in two days. He was confident his arm was ready for Seneca, and ready for the season.

Boy, is it ready, Alex thought after a few minutes of throwing. She could feel it every time he buried another fastball in the pocket of her catcher's mitt.

By the end of their session, having limited himself to just thirty throws, Gabe was feeling so good about himself that he started showing off different arm angles. When he called his last pitch, he told Alex to stay loose, because he was coming at her sidearm.

The ball flew toward Alex from where third base would have been if she had a real baseball diamond in her yard. But the pitch was wild, forcing her to do a pretty amazing split to come up with the ball, stretching out her arm and catcher's mitt as far as it would go.

"You just saved me from my first wild pitch of the season!" Gabe said, laughing.

"You're welcome!" Alex yelled back, seated in the grass by now.

"You know," Gabe said, coming over to help her up, "you looked like a goalie there. Maybe you've been playing out of position."

"Yeah, right," Alex said. "I'll be happy playing midfield on Saturday."

"Mixing it up on the soccer pitch with Chase Gwinn," Gabe said. "And doing it in front of a big crowd. You ready for that?"

"So ready," Alex said as they walked back into her house.

"Did you ever think when we were playing football that you'd end up here?"

Alex guffawed. "I didn't even know I was going to be playing soccer again!"

They shut the back door and headed into the living room, plopping down on the cushy sofa in front of the TV.

"Hey," Gabe said before Alex clicked on the screen, "a couple of weeks ago, I didn't even know I'd be pitching in our first game."

Alex smiled at her friend. "But you know something?" she said. "We're both in a pretty good place right now."

"Totally," Gabe said. "First big games we've had since football."

41

Gabe left to go home around five thirty, and Alex's mom came over for dinner an hour later.

She sat right down at the kitchen table and dug into the Thai food her dad had ordered from Lemongrass. Alex sat down with her while Jack washed his hands at the sink.

"I found out something today," Liza said out loud.

Technically, she was addressing them both, but it was Alex to whom she gave her full attention. Alex knew her mom well enough by now to know that whatever she was about to say wasn't good.

Alex waited for her to continue.

"I have to go back to San Francisco," she said.

Alex's heart skipped a beat.

"When?" she asked, even though she was pretty sure she already knew the answer.

"Tomorrow," her mom said apologetically.

That's when Alex knew for sure.

"You're going to miss our game," she said.

It wasn't a question. If her mom was leaving tomorrow, Thursday, she'd be away on Saturday.

"One of Richard's patients requires an hours-long surgery," she said. "From what he tells me, it's a complicated procedure, and he'll need to be at the hospital most of the day Saturday."

There had to be more to the story, Alex thought. Richard's job was just as demanding as her mom's. This wasn't exactly new information.

"He's going to be at the hospital all day," Alex's mom went on, "and your brother has his first T-ball game on Saturday. I can't have him there without either one of his parents."

At first, Alex felt a little angry. A T-ball game? For five-year-olds? It would probably last a total of twenty minutes, and anyway, kids that age could hardly make contact with the ball. To fly six hours for such a short, insignificant event seemed a little silly to Alex.

But then she thought about it harder. The truth was, there was no difference between a five-year-old's T-ball game and the World Series. Not when it came to having your loved ones there to support you. Alex remembered her own T-ball games as a kid. Her dad cheering her on from behind the gate. Nothing could replace those memories or the feeling of someone you love backing you up.

In fact, maybe it was even more important for Connor, Alex thought. Having that kind of encouragement from an early age could affect how he viewed sports for the rest of his life.

It finally clicked, and as disappointed as Alex was that her mom would be missing The Game, she knew Connor needed her more this time.

"I'm so sorry, honey," her mom said now. "If there were any possible way to be in two places at once, you know I'd find it."

"I know, Mom," Alex said. "You're Wonder Woman."

"Hardly," Liza said. "Not trying to be a superhero. Just a super mom."

Alex's dad jumped in. "I told your mom I'd get somebody to tape The Game if I have to," he said. "There's even some talk that the school might find a way to livestream it, so that people can purchase digital tickets and watch from home."

"And I told your dad," her mom said, "that it won't be the same."

Alex could see how conflicted her mom felt, as if she were choosing one child over the other. But Alex knew that wasn't the case. She was doing the right thing, and Alex believed it was her job right now not to make her feel worse than she already did.

"Mom, I get it," Alex said. "I know how I would have felt if Dad hadn't been there for my first soccer game all those years ago."

Liza cracked a half smile.

"I'm just sad to be losing part of our team . . ." Alex said jokingly.

"No kidding," her mom said. "Your star page-layer-outer."

Then she turned to Alex's dad and said, "Can you hold off on dessert for a few minutes?"

Jack pressed a hand to his heart in mock horror. "I'll do my best, but you don't know what you're asking."

Liza turned to face Alex then. "Let's you and me have a chat in your room."

"Mom, I'm fine," Alex said. "Really."

"Now, you know neither one of us really is," her mom said. "And you should know that mothers are practically obligated to talk things to death."

• • •

They sat facing each other on Alex's bed, her mom perched at the end, Alex with her back to the headboard, lying among her many pillows.

"I'm flying back as soon as everything's all squared away with Richard's patient," she said. "And if there's a season—scratch that, *when* there's a season—I'll get to see a bunch of games before I'm back home for good."

As great as it had been having her here, it wasn't permanent. No matter how much Alex had tried to pretend, the reality was that this wasn't her mother's home. Not this house. Not Orville. Not anymore.

Home for her was San Francisco.

Home was *there*.

It was always going to *be* there.

"I wish there were another way," Alex said to her. "But we both know there isn't."

Her mom reached over and took both her hands.

"The last time you had a big game," she said, "I was flying east. Coming *to* the game. This time I'm going the other way."

And then Alex told her mom how much it had meant to her to have her around for this long. How they'd made up for lost time, and that even just the dinners the three of them shared made them feel like a real family, at least for a little while.

"Honey," her mom said. "We *are* a real family. And always will be. Just maybe not exactly the way I'd imagined things when I had you."

Alex nodded. "I know I said it like a joke before," she said, "but I meant it when I said you were part of the team."

Liza patted Alex's knee and gave it a little shake. "And I mean it when I say I feel the same way."

Alex got up off the bed and grabbed her phone from her desk. She opened up Spotify and started up her Taylor Swift playlist. During her mom's stay, one of many things they'd discovered was how much they both loved Taylor Swift.

A song started playing through Alex's Bluetooth speakers: "The Best Day."

How ironic, Alex thought. But when she stopped to listen to the lyrics, she realized Taylor was describing her mother. And how she'd been there for her during tough times. Alex's mom might not be there for The Game, but she'd supported Alex her whole life. Even from afar.

"Hey," Alex's mom said now. "You did this, you know? You and the other girls on the team. You turned a good idea into something glorious."

"That's what Coach says."

"Another reason to love that Coach Cross."

"But no matter how great a day it is," Alex said, "how great can it be if we don't end up raising enough money?"

"You will," Liza said. "I have faith."

"But what if we don't, Mom?"

"Then it will *still* be a day to remember," she said. "Your dad's right. There really are all sorts of ways to keep score in sports."

It was quiet between them for a few seconds. Not an awkward quiet. Peaceful, really.

"Since it *is* just us," Alex said, "can I tell you something?"

"Anything."

"I know Saturday is about more than winning The Game," she said. "But I want to beat those guys so bad."

Liza let out a belly laugh that shook the mattress. "That's my girl," she said.

Then her mom got up and threw her arms around Alex. They stayed that way, in a standing hug, neither one moving for a long time, just listening to the music.

42

THE FORECAST PREDICTED THAT SATURDAY WOULD BE ONE OF THE warmest days of the year so far. Even though they hadn't reached the official first day of spring, the temperature was supposed to be in the midsixties.

But today was Friday, and winter was still very much alive and well. Alex sat on the cold bleachers in Seneca with her dad, the two of them bundled under their thick Steelers football blanket. They were ready to watch Gabe's first baseball game of the season on a chilly, sunless afternoon.

Spring training had begun in Florida and Arizona for big-league teams. But this was western Pennsylvania, which meant just-above-freezing temperatures and gray skies.

The game took place at a cool baseball park near the center of town, with an outfield fence covered in advertisements from local businesses. Alex looked at them with a tinge of regret for not setting their sights wider by approaching stores in neighboring towns for their program, but at this point, it didn't matter. They had been able to fill up the program just fine from Orville businesses alone.

As cold as she was, even underneath the black-and-yellow knit blanket she and her dad used for Steelers games in December and January, she was glad to be at Gabe's game today, seeing her friend preparing to throw his first pitches of the season in the bottom of the first.

And yet, right at this very moment, her mom was boarding a flight from Pittsburgh's airport to San Francisco International.

The only other people in the stands on the third-base side were parents of the Orville players. Before the Owls had batted in the top of the first, Gabe had come over to where they were sitting.

"You came," he said to Alex.

"A promise is a promise," she reminded him, "even if I feel like I'm going to be watching you from inside a refrigerator."

"Thanks for coming anyway," Gabe said.

"I tell you all the time," Alex said, "you'd do the same for me."

"Now I just need to throw as well to Cal as I do in your backyard," Gabe said.

Cal was Cal Calabrese, Dr. Calabrese's son. He played on the Owls football team and was also Gabe's catcher.

"You bring home a *W* today," Alex said, "and then our team will get one tomorrow."

"Thinking positive?" Gabe asked.

"Yeah," Alex said. "Me and the girls are like the Little Engine That Could."

Gabe laughed. *"You think you can. You think you can."*

"Exactly." Then Alex pulled her hand out from underneath the blanket and high-fived him. "And today, I *know* you can."

The Owls jumped off to a lead in their first at-bat, thanks to three of Alex's football teammates. Tariq Connolly, a center-fielder, hit a double that rolled all the way to the outfield fence, right in front of a sign for Cold Stone. Gabe was next up, batting third because he was their best hitter, and he singled home Tariq. It was 1–0, just like that. Then big Perry Moses, who'd been a clutch tight end for Alex, doubled home Gabe, and by the time the half inning was over, the Owls led, 2–0.

Then it was time for Gabe to take the mound and pitch a real game for the first time since he played for the sixth-grade team last spring. Alex studied his face and body language for signs of nerves but couldn't spot any, though she was positive he had to be feeling *something*.

And he promptly proved it by walking the Bears' leadoff batter on four straight pitches, not one of them close to being a strike.

He slipped on his first pitch to their second batter and went down.

Alex gasped, a little too loudly, and her father gently placed a hand on her arm to calm her.

"Relax, kid," he said. "I think he just stepped in a hole the other pitcher made with his landing foot. It rained yesterday, remember? That dirt in front of the mound looks pretty soft to me."

Jack had once been a pitcher himself, back when he was at Orville High. It turned out he knew what he was talking about, because Gabe popped right back up, waved off his coach and Cal, cleaned off the front of his pants, and then used his spikes to smooth out the area where he wanted to land in front of the mound.

When he got back to work, he struck out the batter on his next three pitches, then proceeded to strike out the next two batters after him to end the inning.

"Knee looks strong enough to me," her dad said.

"Not as strong as his arm," Alex remarked.

"Looks like the old Gabe is back."

"Or the new and improved Gabe . . ."

Before the game, Gabe assumed the most he might pitch today was three innings. It wasn't ideal baseball weather, it was his first start of the season, and he didn't expect to throw more than forty pitches. But Alex was keeping count and knew it was still low after Tariq dropped a ball in centerfield that allowed the Bears to score two runs in the bottom of the second inning.

It was still 2–2 in the fourth when Gabe led off with a single and then, showing no fear about his knee, stole second base, sliding in there hard. Perry struck out after that. So did Liam Goldstein, their second baseman.

But then Cal singled sharply to left field, and Alex knew that with two outs, Gabe would try to go all the way and score the go-ahead run. She forgot about the blanket and stood up as Gabe rounded third, watching the Bears left fielder charge the ball and pick it up cleanly and come up throwing.

Then her eyes moved back to Gabe, closing in on home base, running as fast as if he were on a football field.

Good as new.

The play was right in front of her. She could see Gabe and caught sight of the ball, bouncing about twenty feet in front of the Seneca catcher but right on line.

Clearly it was going to be a close play at the plate.

The Seneca catcher readied himself to take the throw.

"He's going to slide right into him," Alex whispered.

Defending Champ

She wasn't talking to her dad, just herself. The throw had been wide when Gabe had stolen second, so there was no one on the base when he went sliding in there.

This was different.

And this was Gabe, going into his slide as the catcher reached up to glove the ball.

His bad knee hit the ground first, in what appeared to Alex like a perfect slide. Dirt sprayed everywhere as the catcher tried to block the plate with one of his knees and simultaneously put a sweep tag on Gabe.

The tag was late.

The home plate umpire signaled that Gabe was safe.

As he did, Gabe rolled over onto his back, but only for an instant.

Alex watched then as he sprung to his feet, a huge smile spread across his face.

He turned toward the stands and pointed at her.

She smiled and pointed back.

It was 3–2, Owls.

Gabe got to stay out there and pitch the bottom of the fourth, got three more outs before his coach brought in the Owls' relief pitcher, another football teammate, Jake Caldwell. He pitched as well as Gabe did, all the way until the final out of the game.

Owls 3, Bears 2.

Final.

Gabe was the winning pitcher. Jake got the save. When it was over, after the two teams met in the middle of the diamond to shake hands, Gabe walked back over to Alex and her dad, who'd made their way down through the bleachers.

205

She gave him one more high five.

"Tell the truth," Gabe said. "I scared you with that slide into home."

"Who, me?" Alex said, trying to sound innocent. "Not even a little bit."

Gabe gave her a little shove. "That run won us the game," he said.

"Whatever it takes," Alex said.

"I got my game," Gabe said. "Now it's your turn."

43

IT WAS JUST ALEX AND HER DAD FOR DINNER ON FRIDAY NIGHT after they got home from Seneca.

Just the two of them, like most nights.

Except tonight wasn't most nights.

When they sat down, Alex had just gotten off the phone with Lindsey, who'd spoken to Coach Cross just a few minutes earlier.

"Lindsey doesn't think we're going to make it to twenty-five thousand," Alex said.

Even now, the number sounded odd to her. She'd never really thought about a sum of money that large in her life.

"She may think that," Jack said. "But she's got no way of knowing it."

"She's the one who called Coach, who's got all the numbers, at least so far," Alex said.

"No way Coach Cross would have said that to Lindsey."

"She didn't," Alex said. "Lindsey sort of came to that conclusion on her own."

He grinned. "I'm glad you and Lindsey are getting along now," he said. "But that girl can be a little over the top."

"She thinks we're basically going to have to sell out everything tomorrow to get anywhere close," Alex said. "Shirts, hats, snacks, beverages, everything."

They were having turkey burgers tonight, a dish her dad had been perfecting all winter. He said they were healthier than beef burgers, which was fine with Alex because they tasted even better. For dessert, they'd stopped on the way home to pick up an apple pie at Babinksy's, their local bakery famous for their pies.

"Let me ask you a question," Jack said. "Is there anything else you could have done? And when I say 'you,' I mean all of you girls."

Alex shook her head. "Nope," she said. "Nobody on our team could have worked any harder. Even Rashida's still killing it on social media after coming down with strep."

"Kind of knew the answer before I asked," he said. "My point being, I know you all did your best."

"With the number of players and opinions on our team," Alex said, "it could have turned into a disaster. But everybody came together."

"You worked hard, you acted as a team, and you had a ton of fun along the way," he said. "That's some season you've had right there."

"*Had?*" Alex said.

"Slow down," he said. "I'm not saying this thing is over. I'm just trying to tell you that whatever happens tomorrow, you've had yourself a time. And I don't think any of you would have missed this ride for anything. Am I right?"

"You're always right."

He snickered. "Hardly."

"I just don't want it to end, Dad."

"What do we always say? Control what you can control," he

said. "In other words, go out there tomorrow and have a blast knowing you're playing in the most famous soccer match to happen in Orville, Pennsylvania."

Alex nodded, taking a bite of her turkey burger.

"And think about this," he added. "The day is almost here, and not once have we discussed winning or losing against the boys."

Alex leaned forward. "Can I make a confession?"

"The floor is yours."

"I sure am thinking about it!" she said.

"You wouldn't be Alexandra Carlisle if you weren't," he said. "And I don't say it as often as I should, but I'm proud of you, kiddo."

"Dad," Alex teased, "you tell me practically every day."

"Well, that's still not often enough," he said. "And today I'm even prouder than usual. Because these girls were the ones who lined up against you last fall, and now here you are a few months later lining up *with* them, leading the charge."

"It wasn't just me."

"I know that," he said. "But whether it's about playing quarterback for the football team or trying to save the girls' soccer season, you set your mind on a goal and never let anything stop you."

"It worked out well for football," Alex said. "But the jury's still out on soccer . . ."

"If the worst happens and you don't end up raising enough money," he said, "then you might as well go out there and win the sucker and soak up all the glory."

"You really think we have a chance?" she said.

"It's like the great basketball coach Jim Valvano said the day before North Carolina State played in the championship game. People kept telling him they didn't have a chance, and Jimmy V. said, 'There's only two teams left. I *gotta* have some kind of chance.' And you know how that game turned out . . ."

She did know. North Carolina State won the game on a basket right before the buzzer.

Alex sighed now, releasing more air than she was taking in. "You never told me seventh grade was going to be this complicated," she said.

"If I did," he said, "I would have had to preface it with a spoiler alert."

They ate their slices of apple pie with vanilla ice cream. Once they'd finished, Alex's dad told her he'd handle the cleanup so Alex could have some alone time.

"Am I that obvious?" she asked.

"Just to a veteran observer like myself," he said, winking at his only daughter. "Sometimes seventh graders aren't nearly as complicated as they think they are."

She went up to her room and took a very hot shower. The chill from sitting through Gabe's baseball game hadn't totally worn off. But she was so happy for Gabe. On their way home, her dad had told her it was another game that might not have happened without her influence.

"He's Gabe," Alex had said. "He would have found his way there on his own."

Her dad had peered at her through the rearview mirror. "But it pays to have friends who care about you."

Alex flopped onto her bed, cuddling up with Simba, her lucky charm, and tried to read the new book assigned to her English class called *Hoot* by Carl Hiaasen.

As much as she'd been enjoying the book so far, she couldn't wrap her head around the words tonight. They blurred on the page whenever she tried to concentrate, and her brain couldn't focus on stringing the sentences together.

She slid off her bed, walked over to her dresser, and smiled at what was sitting on top.

The custom T-shirt and hat her mom had bought her for The Game, plus a copy of the program they'd worked on together.

She flipped open to the first page of the program and noticed something she hadn't before.

A note addressed to her.

It was from her mom.

Alex could tell who wrote it just by the "doctor scrawl" handwriting that even on Liza's best day was barely legible.

But it was legible enough for her daughter.

Us girls are allowed to have it all.
Love,
Mom

44

COACH CROSS HAD A PRETTY COOL OPENING LINE FOR THEM WHEN the team gathered in the gym together an hour before The Game.

"For the next couple of hours," she said, "you're not sales-people, or editors, or social media managers. You're soccer players."

"'Curadh' is a word they use for a group like this back home," Roisin said.

She looked around at her teammates' blank faces.

"Warriors," she explained.

The weather forecasters were right. It was a perfect outdoor day. For soccer or just about anything. But it was inside where the day was about to get even better.

Coach walked them over to two huge boxes set underneath one of the baskets and showed them their new uniforms.

They even had their names on the backs to go with the numbers.

"These," she said, "are a gift from me and my husband to all of you. You've never asked for anything throughout this entire process. And whatever happens today, you deserve these."

They were white with blue and red trim, modeled after the ones the US women's national team had worn when they won their last World Cup.

As the girls tore through the boxes, finding their jerseys, Coach said to Alex, "Be a shame to only wear them once, wouldn't you agree?"

"Totally," Alex said.

The stands were already full by the time they got outside to warm up, everybody feeling fresh in their new jerseys.

Alex noticed Jabril near the gate, selling tickets as fans came pouring in. Sophie was working the concession stand with some of the cheerleaders, handing out hot dogs, lemonades, and sodas. Some of the soccer moms, all wearing The Game T-shirts, walked up and down the stands, selling game-day merchandise and passing out programs.

Alex took in the whole scene. It was like something out of an episode of *Friday Night Lights*. Fans crowding the bleachers, foam fingers waving in the air, the smell of popcorn wafting over the field.

The girls marveled at the spectacle, almost unbelieving that everyone was there to witness them play. To witness Orville history being made.

Somebody had set up signs on either side of the field, ones the girls hadn't arranged. A bunch of local businesses. Sam's and Bostwick's Ice Cream and the Candy Kitchen Deli and Old Town Bagels. All wanting to show their last-minute support of The Game. Alex wondered when those deals had been arranged, but there wasn't any time to concern herself with that now.

The Orville YMCA had the biggest signs of the lot, set up behind both goals.

They read this way, in huge letters:

GO TEAM(S).

There was no designated home side or visitors' side in the bleachers. This was an all-Orville crowd today, whether they were rooting for the boys or girls or had just come to see a good game.

Despite what Coach had said about only needing to make $5,000 today to reach their goal, Alex found herself sneaking looks at the concessions booth and the table where Gabe and his mom were selling gear, just to see what the lines looked like.

First we're going to have a final score on the field, she thought. *Then the final tally when The Game is over.*

At one point, Roisin nudged her in the side. "Quit lookin' over there and get yer focus back here."

"Roger that," Alex said.

Coach gathered them around her on the sideline at five minutes to one.

"I'm going to tell you something that coaches have said to underdog teams for a long time," she said. "Maybe the boys would beat us nine games out of ten. But we're not playing them ten times. We're playing them once. Just once. All we have to do is beat them today."

Alex thought to herself: *We can say the score doesn't matter, but we'd only be fooling ourselves. In sports, everything changes when you're keeping score for real.*

"I don't want you to dwell on our scrimmage against them

all those weeks ago," Coach continued. "But I do want you to remember how it ended. Because *that*, girls, is who we are."

She put her hand out. They crowded close to her and put their hands in on top of hers.

As far as who would be starting, Coach Cross assured them they'd all get their minutes. But for today she was going with Annie, Lindsey, Roisin, and Alex up front.

"My fab front four," she said.

Alex wore No. 13, Alex Morgan's number on the national team and in the Olympics. Alex Carlisle hadn't asked for the number, because she hadn't known they were getting uniforms. Coach had come up with the idea herself.

"I gave you that number for a reason," she said to Alex. "Now get out there and play like her."

Alex ran out onto the field with her teammates and took midfield.

Then she took it upon herself before the teams lined up to go over and shake Chase's hand.

"Glad you could make it," Alex said.

"You know something?" Chase said. "So am I."

"May the best team win," Alex said. "That's a thing people say, right?"

Before Chase turned away, he said, "We already know who the best team is."

It was classic Chase Gwinn, but the way he said it was friendlier. More in the spirit of a good rivalry. Alex caught herself smiling as she backed up into position.

Both teams were tight at the start. For the boys, it may have been because they didn't dominate the first few minutes like they had during the scrimmage. The high school scoreboard towered over the field, showing four minutes in when Chase missed a wide-open shot, even with Carly out of position, blasting one wide off the far post.

Then, about a minute later, Alex blew her own chance to get the girls on the scoreboard first, despite a very fancy pass from Roisin. She had room in the near corner, plenty of room, because the boys' keeper, Danny Stroud, had been playing Roisin to shoot. But Alex took too much time, Danny got back into the play, and when she finally did shoot the ball, he got a hand on it and deflected it over the crossbar.

Still 0–0.

They would hear it from the crowd every time someone on either team made a nice play on offense or defense. Or when the keepers made a good save.

Despite Afafa's scoring skills, Coach had put her in as a defender today, and she was proving herself to be just as strong in that position, working together with Maria and Carly to protect the goal.

At one point Alex thought, *This has to be the biggest crowd to ever watch a soccer game in Orville.*

It was an amazing game so far. After all the trash talk leading up to today, there was hardly any of that now. They were all too busy trying to win a game.

The boys scored first.

It was partially Alex's fault. Not because of the way the play ended, but the way it began. And the way it began was Chase taking the ball away from her without much difficulty.

Alex had just seen what she thought was an opening for herself down the right side, with both Roisin and Annie running down the middle of the field, slightly ahead of her. But then Alex made the one mistake she'd been telling herself all week she couldn't make in this game:

She lost sight of Chase.

He was behind her and to her left, almost like a pass rusher in football coming from her blind side as Alex pushed the ball ahead of her at full speed.

And then, without warning, the ball was gone.

Chase, having made his move, spun lightning-fast in the other direction, slipping past one defender after another. Johnny Gallotta tried to catch up with him, running on Chase's left. Then suddenly they crisscrossed, anticipating each other's moves. Johnny ran at Carly. Chase was over to her right.

Alex ran as hard as she could to catch up with them and get back into the play.

Too late, though. She watched as Chase came to a dead stop in front of Maria. Then he started up again. Then another stop. Finally, he cut around her, carrying the ball the way he had for fifty yards, never once looking down to see where the ball was.

Because he knew.

It was *his* ball.

His game right now.

Alex finally caught up, and now she and Maria tried to double-team him.

For a blink, they seemed to have him covered.

But he spun one more time and was gone.

Carly came up and tried to cut off his angle to the goal. Only it was here that Chase made one of the coolest moves Alex had ever seen, with only five yards separating him from Carly.

He elevated the ball with his right foot, straight up into the air, essentially making a pass to himself, before heading it over Carly's left shoulder and into the net behind her.

Alex could hear the biggest explosion yet from the crowd, and Alex fought the urge to applaud along with them. She didn't much care for Chase as a person, but as a player? He was a total star. Her favorite player in the men's Premier League was Harry Kane of Tottenham. Chase played the game like him.

And now the score was 1–0.

All week long Alex had hoped that the people who'd bought tickets to The Game would feel as if they were getting the show they deserved.

They were sure getting that now.

"You're going to wish you'd stuck with football," Chase said as he ran past her, just loud enough for Alex to hear. "Out here, *I'm* the quarterback."

But somehow, after just one score, it was Alex and her teammates who raised their game, from the time Chase put the ball behind Carly until the end of the half. Coach had been stressing, at every practice, that defense and not offense would win this game, especially taking Chase's knack for scoring into consideration.

"The best form of attacking," she kept telling them, "is defense."

That's what the girls were doing now, playing their zones, not taking reckless chances when they had the ball, and doing their best to play keep-away in their own end when they could. They played cautiously, waiting for a good opening to advance, as if they all knew the worst possible thing would be to fall two goals behind before halftime.

At a minute left in the half, they took the play to the boys' end of the field. Alex could see the boys suddenly playing tight again, knowing that as good as their keeper, Danny Stroud, had played so far, one mistake or one good shot could tie The Game. They couldn't have expected The Game to be this close, not after what they'd done to the girls in their scrimmage.

But here we are, Alex thought.

And we're not going anywhere.

"I don't care how good you are," Jack liked to say. "You don't want to let the other team hang around."

The girls didn't score before the half. Annie put a terrific shot on Danny with twenty seconds left, but he made an even better save. The game stayed at 1–0, boys.

At halftime Lindsey said, "We can take these guys."

"We *will* take these guys," Alex said, surprising herself with how forcefully the words came out.

Sophie had come walking over from where she and the other cheerleaders were taking their halftime break and heard Roisin say to Alex, "You sound pretty sure about us."

Sophie grinned and poked Roisin with an elbow from behind. "You're about to find out that good teams follow my friend Alex around."

Annie came over and put her arm in the air, waving them all

in. Soon, they all had their arms in the air, meeting Annie's.

"Alex is right," Annie said with conviction. "We are *going* to take these guys."

As they walked back onto the field, Alex took another glance toward the concessions booth and the nearby table selling shirts and hats. She was happy to see long lines. But Coach was right. There was nothing any of them could do about money now.

All they could do, for themselves, was win The Game.

Less than a minute into the second half, Carly kept The Game at 1–0 by making a ridiculous save on Chase after Johnny Gallotta had set him up with a sweet long pass. Chase didn't have a lot of time but still tried to fake Carly, at least to get her leaning right. But Carly didn't bite and remained vigilant, waiting for Chase to make *his* move. When he did, he pounded a shot to her left, but Carly had read him perfectly, maybe closer to the post than she thought, and tipped the ball with her fingertips.

For one agonizing moment, Alex thought she might have deflected the ball to the inside of the post, and into the goal.

She hadn't.

The ball went wide.

Still 1–0.

It was frustrating that they couldn't break through. But Alex could sense Chase, more than anyone else, getting increasingly irritated. Even with the lead, he wasn't satisfied, as if annoyed the boys weren't up by more at this point.

Alex thought if he kept trying to do too much, he would eventually make a mistake.

With eight minutes left, that's exactly what he did.

Carrying the ball again near midfield, he should have passed it to Johnny, who was wide open. But he didn't. Selfishly, he held on to the ball, attempting to make another hero play, dazzle everybody again, split Alex and Roisin one more time.

They didn't let him.

Maybe they knew they *couldn't* let him, not this late in The Game.

Alex stripped him cleanly.

Picked his pocket, as Coach liked to say.

As she traveled down the field, she heard Chase from behind saying, *"What the heck?"*

The play turned around so quickly that the closest defenders were backing up as she approached. She was the attacker now.

She had Roisin to her left, Lindsey to her right.

Annie was trailing the play.

"Right behind you," Alex heard Annie say.

The fab front four. Doing their thing.

They were finally past every defender except one. Charlie Cooper. Their best. Good guy. *Really* good player.

He put all of his focus on Alex, who still had the ball.

Waiting for her to make *her* move.

Looking right at Lindsey, Alex pushed the ball to her left, over to Roisin. She'd hoped Charlie would go for her fake, but he didn't. He went with Roisin. Only now Roisin didn't hesitate.

The ball came right back to Alex.

Danny had moved when Alex had made her initial pass to Roisin, covering any angle Roisin had to his short side. Only now he had to scramble back to the middle of the goal.

Too late.

Alex buried her shot behind him, the ball hitting the net so hard Alex thought it might take the whole goal down with it. Hardest shot of her life.

Now The Game was tied.

45

IT HAD LONG SINCE BEEN DECIDED THAT THEY WEREN'T GOING TO play an overtime or decide The Game on penalty kicks. They were treating it like one of those "friendly" international matches between countries, one in which the outcome never showed up in anybody's standings. This wasn't a playoff game. Wasn't for the championship of any league.

But it felt like one.

Alex knew there wasn't a single player out there who wanted this game to end in a tie, even though the people watching would probably consider it a victory for everyone if it did.

She wanted to beat these guys.

So did her teammates. Especially now that they'd evened the score.

With two minutes left, the refs blew their whistles for a time-out.

Alex ran down in front of Carly and motioned for her teammates to follow her.

"I know I don't have to say this, but I'm going to anyway," she said. "If this *is* the only game we get to play this season, we are *not* losing it."

It was clear the boys wanted the win just as much as they did. Right after The Game resumed, Chase found himself at the top of the circle in front of Carly, and without hesitating, he kicked the ball so screamingly hard that Alex thought it should have been trailed by a jet stream.

A shot headed for the upper corner.

Alex had always thought one of the best things about sports was when you did something you didn't know you could. Made a play you didn't know you had in you.

Carly Jones made one now.

She flew to her left and was up and off the ground, chasing the ball toward the corner. Then, miraculously, she was soaring through the air, her arm extending out.

Not only did she get her gloved left hand on the ball.

She *caught* it.

Then she landed back on the ground and rolled the ball to Maria, her closest teammate, who sent it back up the field to Alex.

Alex gave a quick look at the scoreboard at the other end of the field.

One minute.

She was in the boys' end then, with Lindsey, Roisin, and Annie spreading the field. Fab four, on one more rush, maybe their last for the day.

Alex still had the ball. She sent it over to Annie. Got it back. Then kicked it over to Roisin.

Back to Alex.

Everything happened in quick succession, the boys defending them just trying to keep up.

The ball was moving faster than they could.

After the last time-out, the refs had informed both teams that they wouldn't be putting any extra time on the clock to reflect stoppages in play. And that when the time on the clock expired, when the scoreboard said 0:00, The Game was over.

Had to be under thirty seconds now, Alex told herself.

Now or never.

Roisin and Annie spread out wider, just to give the defenders something to think about, making sure they weren't offsides inside the key.

Charlie Cooper was left to cover both Alex and Lindsey.

Charlie wasn't messing around. He'd seen the whole game. Seen what Alex could do. He was staying with her, moving up on her now, crowding her, trying to get her off the ball.

Fat chance.

Alex put on the brakes. This time, she threw caution to the wind, not worrying who might be behind her, and wound up like she was ready to blast one harder than she had on her goal.

Right foot all the way.

Charlie went into a slide, arms behind him, making sure that if he did block the shot before it got to Danny he couldn't get called for a hand ball.

But Charlie forgot something.

Alex was a quarterback.

Quarterbacks pass.

She went with her backyard move. As her right leg started forward, she gently pushed the ball with the side of her left to Lindsey.

Former nemesis. Now trusted teammate.

Then she watched as Lindsey scored the goal that secured them the victory.

Two hours later they were back at Lindsey's house when Coach Cross came in with the final numbers.

"I couldn't be prouder of this team," she said as everyone settled onto Lindsey's living room floor. "And before we get to the numbers, I want you all to take a moment to recognize yourselves for what you accomplished today. Not just the win. But coming together as a team to make this game happen. You put in the work and pulled off an amazing event, and that deserves a round of applause."

The girls clapped and hollered, and all the parents sitting on the couch and standing around the room cheered their heads off. Everyone was still charged up from the win.

Alex's heart was pounding. It *had* been an amazing event, and she'd had the time of her life playing against the guys. But she worried: Would it be enough?

"I want you all to remember this day for the rest of your lives," Coach said. "Even though, I'm sorry to tell you, we came up twenty-five hundred dollars short of our goal."

The room grew instantly silent, and the mood among the girls and their parents dipped from the highest high to the lowest low.

"I wish I had better news," Coach said.

"Good news for our charities," Lindsey said, a little deflated but also hopeful.

From the start, they'd decided if they couldn't raise the full amount they needed, they would distribute the money to local causes in need: a home for the elderly, a rehab facility, an animal shelter, and a struggling church.

"You guys did everything you possibly could," Coach said, "just like you brought it on that field today."

Lindsey piped up again. "Should have found somebody to donate a thousand dollars per goal."

"We still would have come up short," Carly pointed out.

"I refuse to believe this is over," Annie said. "There's gotta be another way to raise the rest of the money."

"We got every dollar out of our town," Alex said. "We just didn't get enough."

The girls vowed to celebrate their victory anyhow, with cake and ice cream and cookies and an impressive fruit platter assembled by Mrs. Stiles. Everything was set up buffet style on their console in the dining room.

When they were all seated with their plates in their laps, and the parents were sipping their coffees, Alex's dad stood up to address the room.

"I tell my daughter something all the time," Jack said. "At the end of the day, sports is a memory-making business. And today, you made one for yourselves, and for all of us."

He raised his coffee mug in a toast.

"And not just on the field," he added.

The spirits in the room lifted a bit after that. Alex blamed it on the sugar, but it was also fun to rehash all the best plays from The Game, like the highlight reels on ESPN. As disappointed as the girls were that their season was not to be, they tried focusing on the positives. Namely, their epic win today.

Then, out of nowhere, the doorbell rang. Alex scanned the room for anyone who might be missing, but the entire team was accounted for, save Rashida, who was home recuperating.

Lindsey got up and walked toward the front door.

When she opened it, Chase and Johnny Gallotta were standing on her porch.

Chase was the one with the check in his hand.

47

He handed the check to Lindsey.

"This is from the guys and me," he said.

As far as Alex knew from personal experience, Lindsey Stiles had never been at a loss for words.

But she was now.

She stared at the check and then back at Chase and Johnny before the three of them walked into the living room.

Lindsey handed the check over to Alex.

When she looked down and saw that it was made out to "Cash," in the amount of $5,000, she covered her mouth in shock.

"How?" Alex finally managed.

"You know those signs at The Game today?" Johnny said. "The guys on the team got together and went to Sam's and Bostwick's and all those places and asked if they'd want to advertise on the field in addition to the ads they'd already purchased in your program."

"Ten of them," Chase said. "Five hundred dollars apiece."

"What made you guys do it?" Alex asked.

Chase managed a grin. "Ask him," he said, nodding over at Jabril, who was seated on the couch with a piece of cake as big as a soccer ball.

"Aw," Jabril said, "all's I did was explain a few things to my man Chase on the phone the other day."

"J told me that it was time for me to get into the game, and not just The Game," Chase said.

He put air quotes around the last two words.

"Told you I know how to get the word out," Jabril said with a wink.

"Anyway," Johnny said, "that's when we got to work, knowing we didn't have much time. We did it on the down-low, kinda wanting it to be a surprise."

He grinned sheepishly.

"And thinking it would make you guys feel better after we beat you," he added with a hint of embarrassment. "So much for that."

Alex laughed. "You have to admit, though, it was a great game."

Chase sighed, then nodded. "Where'd you come up with that move on the winning goal?"

"I saw you do it in a game last season," Alex said, and Chase's cheeks went pink.

Then she explained to him and Johnny how they'd come up short in their fundraising, but now, thanks to them, they had $2,500 more than they needed.

"What should we do with the extra cash?" Annie asked.

"Pretty sure those charities are still in need," Lindsey said.

"Win-win," said Alex.

"More like win-win-win," said Chase.

Sophie came over then, squeezing herself next to Alex. "Got

any room for one more win?" she said. "I just found out we made the cut. We're going to nationals!"

Alex turned and hugged her friend fiercely. "Never had any doubt," she said.

The noise and laughter resumed, and while twenty minutes ago it felt as though the roof had collapsed on them, now, Alex thought, they were raising it.

Five minutes into their arrival, Chase slapped his forehead, saying he'd forgotten that a bunch of other guys from the team were waiting outside for him and Johnny. Lindsey told him to invite them inside, and so the party expanded.

It was still early in the evening, so a bunch of the kids from both teams ran out into Lindsey's backyard for a coed impromptu scrimmage. They mixed the teams up, so now Lindsey was playing with Chase, and Annie and Johnny paired up against them.

Between the soccer being played outside, second helpings of dessert, and constant chatter about The Game, the night sped by, and soon it was time for everyone to go home.

Before Chase left, he pulled Alex aside by the stairs and said, "Think you might want to join *another* boys' team next fall?"

They didn't notice Gabe behind them.

"Stay away from my quarterback," he said.

LATER ON, AFTER ALEX AND HER DAD DROVE HOME, SHE FOUND herself alone in her room, on her bed with Simba.

The game ball sat between them. Alex had refused to take it at first. She'd tried to hand the ball right over to Lindsey, but she wouldn't take it. Neither would Carly. They finally reached a compromise and said they would pass it around the way hockey players did with the Stanley Cup. Their win was a team effort, after all. Alex didn't feel she deserved all the credit.

Her phone started buzzing then, and she checked the screen: MOM.

"You finally stop celebrating?" Liza said.

"It was more exhausting than playing The Game!" Alex joked.

Her mom had already talked to her dad, who'd sent along some clips of The Game, including bonus footage he'd taken of Chase arriving with the $5,000 check.

"Mom," she said, "at the end it was as if we were all on the same team."

"And at that point you probably thought the day couldn't get any better," her mom said.

There was a pause, and then Alex said, "Thanks for the note."

"Turned out to be prophetic, right?" her mom said. "Sometimes we *do* get to have it all."

There was another pause. But even with the distance between them, Alex felt as if her mom were right here in the room with her, sitting at the edge of her bed.

"So I have to ask," her mom said. "What's next?"

"Something I've been waiting a long time to say," Alex said.

"And what's that?"

"Next Saturday's game."